ATTACK BY SKY PIRATES!

Crash!

Glass flew from the front of the plane; the wind howled. Jonny looked forward to the cockpit and saw China Bill wrestling with two sky-pirates, who were climbing through the smashed side window of the cockpit.

Dr. Quest ran forward to help.

"Stop them!" Jessie shouted.

A sky-pirate, complete with headband and a knife in his teeth, leaped through the open cargo door; he was followed by another.

Jonny Quest was knocked backward, off his feet.

"Woof, woof" yelped Bandit, leaping at the intruders' throats. Fists flew and knives flashed. The plane rocked and rolled in the clouds—no one was at the controls!

Read all of
The Real Adventures of Jonny Quest™
books

The Demon of the Deep
The Forbidden City of Luxor
The Pirates of Cyber Island
Peril in the Peaks
*Evil Under the Ice**
*The Monsters From Beyond Time**

by Brad Quentin

*coming soon

JONNY QUEST
THE REAL ADVENTURES

PERIL IN THE PEAKS

BRAD QUENTIN

HarperPrism

An Imprint of HarperPaperbacks

▆ HarperPaperbacks

A Division of HarperCollins*Publishers*

10 East 53rd Street, New York, N.Y. 10022-5299

This is a work of fiction. The characters, incidents, and dialogues are products of the author's imagination and are not to be construed as real. Any resemblance to actual events or persons, living or dead, is entirely coincidental.

ISBN 0-06-105718-5

HarperPrism is an imprint of HarperPaperbacks.

HarperCollins®, ▆ ®, and HarperPaperbacks™, and HarperPrism® are trademarks of HarperCollins*Publishers,* Inc.

Cover illustration © 1996 Hanna-Barbera Productions, Inc.

First printing: December 1996

Printed in the United States of America

Visit HarperPaperbacks on the World Wide Web at
http://www.harpercollins.com/paperbacks

❖ 10 9 8 7 6 5 4 3 2 1

For Caitlin,
who made it all happen

PERIL IN THE PEAKS

1

IT WAS A COLD, CLEAR DAY HIGH ABOVE THE HILLS OF northern Burma. Far below, the land was wrapped in thick, steamy jungle, but up here, at almost twenty thousand feet, it was always cold.

The twin-engine Short droned along with both its turboprops humming.

The two men in the cockpit were both young. The pilot at the controls wore a baseball cap; his companion wore a turban.

"There are the Himalayas, Singh," the pilot said. He pointed toward snow-capped peaks on the northern horizon. "It was in a remote pass called Cloud Alley that I saw the ghost plane."

His copilot laughed. "You're too superstitious, Drew," he said. "Just because the plane seemed to appear out of nowhere doesn't make it a ghost."

The two men were opposites, but alike. Singh had been raised in a religious family, who had hoped he might become a holy man. Instead, he had gone to Scotland to study science and engineering. Drew, a Scot from Glasgow, had been a pilot for several years when he had been drawn to the mystic secrets of the East.

While flying for Felix Air, the two had become fast friends. Since they were both expert pilots, they rarely got to fly together. This flight was a special occasion, though. Singh, who usually flew a different route, had been asked to come along on his day off to help his friend solve a mystery.

"You'll see what I mean by 'ghost plane,'" said Drew. The wiry young Scot held the controls with steady, practiced ease. At twenty-eight he was already a veteran on this route.

"I'll believe it when I see it," Singh said.

"Hang on, skeptic!" Grinning, Drew pushed the throttles forward and threw the plane into a sharp bank, turning toward the ice-covered wall of mountains. There were no passengers on board to complain. Felix Air was a cargo airline. Today they were carrying drums of oil and engine parts.

"If you are trying to scare me, you're wasting your time," Singh said. "Don't forget, I've been flying just as long as you."

Still grinning, Drew leveled the little twin-engine plane. The Short was a favorite of them both. Made in Northern Ireland, it was a practical design: a boxy, high-wing monoplane, roomy, reliable, and capable of landing almost anywhere.

"I'm going to head up Cloud Alley toward the high peaks," Drew said. "The last time I was here, the ghost plane appeared out of those clouds."

"You keep saying *ghost*. What makes you think it was a ghost?"

"For one thing, it was an old plane. A Dakota."

The Dakota was the British name for the twin-engine DC–3, one of the first all-metal cargo planes. It was the backbone of the U.S. and Allied air service during World War II.

Fifty years ago!

"That doesn't make it a ghost," said Singh. "There are a lot of DC–3s still flying. It was a pretty sturdy airplane. Almost as good as the Short. In fact, I've flown a few myself. Why I—"

"There!"

Singh was cut off by Drew's words. Drew tipped the plane into a bank and pointed out the window.

Singh saw a silver twin-engine plane skimming along the tops of the clouds, about a thousand feet below.

"Well, feather my props!" he said. "There it is. It's an old DC–3—a Dakota—just like you said!"

"Just like the one Felix Air lost several years ago. And look, Singh. It seems to be in trouble. It's waggling its wings."

That movement was the international sign of distress.

"Maybe you should fly lower and check it out," said Singh. "I'll see if I can raise it on the radio."

Drew banked steeper and flew down closer to the clouds. The older plane was skimming along with its tail wheel almost touching the tops of the clouds.

"Hello, Dakota!" Singh said, holding the microphone to his lips. "Hello, Dakota. This is the Felix Air Short A786, calling DC–3 in distress! Come in! Come in . . . "

Drew leveled off and throttled back until the Short was following the older plane from slightly above and behind.

3

"He's going up one of the canyons, toward the high peaks," said Drew. "But there's no way through here!" Ahead, through the windscreen, the Himalayas rose like a wall of ice and snow.

Still skimming along the tops of the clouds, the DC–3 turned up a steep valley, and then another. It was like flying through a maze.

"He's going down into the clouds!" said Singh, as the DC–3 banked down.

"Then so are we!" said Drew.

He pushed down the nose of the Short, following. All of a sudden the airplane was wrapped in a white blanket of fog.

"Aren't you afraid we'll hit a peak?" Singh asked.

"According to the map this valley is deep," said Drew. "As long as we don't go any farther north, toward the high peaks, we'll be okay."

"Ease up, we're overtaking them!" Singh yelled.

Drew throttled back and the Short slowed, wallowing in the thin mountain air. The DC–3 was just ahead and slightly above, a ghostly shadow through the clouds.

Suddenly the shadow released more shadows.

"What the—" Drew yelled.

"It looks like men jumping out of the plane!" Singh said.

"They're skydiving toward us!" yelled Drew.

"Pull up!"

"I'm trying!"

The turbines sang and the props dug at the thin air, but too late. There was a series of loud thumps as grappling hooks latched onto the leading edge of the

4

Short's narrow wing. A face appeared at the windscreen—a grinning, bearded pirate face!

BHRUMP!

A small explosion tore open the rear cargo door and cold air filled the plane. Cold air and—shouts and footsteps!

"We've been boarded!" shouted Drew. "Get on the radio! Call . . ."

Singh was putting the microphone to his lips when he felt the cold barrel of a gun against the back of his neck.

"Turn off that radio!" said a heavily accented voice, in perfect English. "And hand me the controls. We are taking command of this aircraft."

2

"WOW!" SAID HADJI. "IT'S 'TERRY AND THE PIRATES!'"

"Who?" asked Jessie and Jonny Quest. The three were hard at work washing the Quest Team's HUMVEE. One of their chores was keeping the equipment clean and in working order.

"At the gate," said Hadji. "Look!"

The three kids turned to see Race Bannon, Jessie's father, welcoming a guest. The stranger had a wide, drooping mustache and wore a leather bomber jacket and a rakish flying cap. He was an old man, but he looked strong and vigorous.

"Didn't you ever read the old comic strip 'Terry and the Pirates?'" Hadji asked. "It was about flyers and adventurers in the Far East. We loved it in India when I was a kid."

"You're still a kid," said Jonny Quest (even though his adopted brother Hadji was a year older than he was), "and I guess I was too busy watching Saturday morning cartoons."

"Who's your father's friend?" Hadji asked Jessie.

"Beats me," said Jessie, the only girl member of the Quest Team. "He's interesting-looking though. Let's go and get nosy!"

6

Seconds later, the HUMVEE was rinsed and the hoses were turned off and put away. The three teens were following Race Bannon and his guest up the stairs of the main house at the center of the Quest compound.

The internationally known explorer and scientist Dr. Benton Quest was in his office studying some maps. The door was open, and even though Jonny, Hadji, and Jessie knew they were welcome at all the meetings of the Quest Team, they hid behind the door.

Sometimes it was more fun to sneak.

"Dr. Quest," Race Bannon was saying, "I'd like you to meet an old friend of mine, Colonel William Sullivan."

"A pleasure," said Dr. Quest. He rose and folded his maps, then pressed the older man's hand warmly. "'China Bill' Sullivan, I believe."

"You've heard of me!" said the guest, surprised.

"Indeed, I have," said Dr. Quest. "You were famous during World War II for helping to pioneer the air route across the mountains from India to Burma. 'Flying the Hump' it was called. Your courageous effort was essential in supplying the Allies and defeating the Japanese.

"They're talking about India!" whispered Hadji. He crept closer to the door. Jonny Quest's adopted brother was always interested in news of his native land.

"World War II was fifty years ago!" whispered Jonny Quest. "This guy is ancient!"

"I didn't do it alone," said Sullivan. "My partner Felix helped pioneer the route. He was the mechanic and I

7

was the pilot. We were a team. Without him, I could never have coaxed those DC-3s over those high peaks."

"Well, it's a pleasure to meet you," said Benton Quest. "Please sit down."

"Colonel Sullivan was briefly called back to active service twenty years ago, to help train some of our S.E.A.L. teams for mountain and jungle warfare," said Race Bannon. "That's when I met him."

"Race and those other kids were pretty good, too," said Sullivan with a twinkle in his eye. "He and I have stayed in touch over the years. Race has told me about the work you and the Quest Team are doing. So when this new problem developed, I thought I might ask you for assistance."

"Problem?" said Dr. Quest. His eyes lit up, as always when he was about to be presented with a new challenge.

"My wartime partner and I shared a dream," said Sullivan. "The two of us planned to start our own airline as soon as the war was over. Then Felix was lost on a flight over the Himalayas, and I did it on my own. I named the airline Felix Air in his honor. It's been pretty successful. We fly cargo in and out of smaller airports in India and Southeast Asia. Then last week I lost a couple of my best pilots and a Short turboprop."

"A crash?" asked Benton Quest.

The old man shook his head. "They went down in an unmapped region hidden under a permanent cloud cover. It's called Cloud Alley. A rival airline lost a couple of DC-3s in that area years ago. The problem is, nobody even knows what's in there under those clouds.

8

That's why I came to you. Race told me you were developing a mapping camera that can penetrate cloud cover."

"True, I have been working on such a device," said Dr. Quest. "The problem is finding a plane that is slow and steady enough for it."

"I can provide just the plane you need," said Sullivan. "And, of course, I will pay all expenses."

"Hmm . . ." Dr. Quest appeared thoughtful. "Well, I suppose that since it *is* an emergency—"

"And it would be an adventure," said Race Bannon.

Three teenage faces peered around the door frame. "What about us?"

"Woof," added Bandit.

China Bill Sullivan turned around in his chair, startled. "We're being spied on!" he said angrily.

"China Bill, meet the rest of our Quest Team," said Dr. Quest. "You kids come on in. Quit hanging out in the doorway like a bunch of hinges. Yes, yes, you can come with us."

Tumbling over one another with excitement, the three youngest members of the Quest Team ran into the room.

"Oh, boy!" said Hadji and Jessie together. "India!"

"When do we go?" Jonny Quest asked his father.

"Tonight!" said the eminent scientist. "Start packing. But first, make sure your chores are done!"

3

TWO DAYS LATER, JONNY AND HADJI WERE SEAT-BELTED TO A bare metal bench, staring out the side window of a vintage DC-3 as it took off over the plains of northern India.

The twin radial engines throbbed with old-fashioned piston power. The silver plane vibrated as it climbed to cruising altitude.

"It's a pleasure to get this old DC-3 out of mothballs," China Bill said, yelling back over his shoulder. "I keep her hangared, oiled, and fueled, but she hasn't been flown in almost ten years, since I replaced all my older planes with Short turboprops. I kept only this one, my favorite."

"It's a beauty," Dr. Benton Quest yelled. He was sitting in the back, across the plane from Jonny and Hadji. Race Bannon and Jessie were forward, in the cockpit with China Bill. Race was in the copilot's seat, and Jessie was behind him, jammed into the tiny corner set aside for the radio operator.

"Fifty-five years ago, when Felix and I were flying the Hump, this plane was state of the art," said China Bill. "After Felix was lost, I started the air cargo business with war surplus DC-3s."

10

"What happened to him?" Race asked.

"I never found out," said China Bill. "It was right before the war ended. He went down in a DC–3 crossing the Himalayas. We searched but we never spotted any wreckage. Soon after, the clouds made the search impossible."

"You mean the clouds hadn't been there before?" asked Jessie.

"Not so thick or so permanent. It was almost as if they were a shroud covering Felix's resting place."

Sadness fell across China Bill's face, like a shadow.

"Well, this DC–3's a beautiful old ship," Dr. Quest said from the back, to cheer him up.

"She's slow and steady," said China Bill. "Which should be perfect for your cloud-penetrating mapping camera. Of course, in the old days the DC–3 didn't seem so slow. A hundred and sixty-five miles per hour was fast!"

Jonny Quest looked out the window. *One hundred and sixty-five mph!* Only yesterday he had been on a jet flying four times as fast. But the sensation was the same. One disappointment about flying was that it never *seemed* fast—since the ground was so far away, it always looked as if they were barely moving. Even a sailboat, with the water rushing past, seemed faster.

Throttling the twin engines back to cruising speed, China Bill leaned back and said: "'Yon sun that sets upon the sea, we follow in his flight!'"

"Huh?" said Race. "Did I miss something?"

"Lord Byron," said Dr. Quest.

11

"Right!" said China Bill with a smile. "A line from my favorite poet. Want to try the controls, Race?"

"You bet," said Bannon. The ex-Navy S.E.A.L.'s seamed face broke into a wide grin. "Haven't flown one of these babies in years." Then he called back, "How do you kids like this plane?"

"It vibrates a lot," said Hadji. "Feels more like a speedboat than an airplane."

"That's because it has piston engines, instead of turbines," said Dr. Quest. He slipped into the "lecture mode" the teens found so amusing. "A jet turbine simply spins. A piston engine has pistons that go up and down, turning a crank that goes around and around. Thus it is converting linear motion to rotary motion, and the vibration represents power lost in the conversion."

"Whatever," said Jonny.

"I think the vibrating is cool," said Jessie. "Sort of like riding on a big Harley-Davidson."

"Exactly!" said Race Bannon, pleased and proud that his daughter understood the thrill of a great machine!

An hour later Jonny saw what he thought was a line of clouds on the horizon.

"There are the clouds you're looking for, Dad," he said, waking up Dr. Benton Quest, who had fallen asleep. The rest of the Quest Team were also sleeping, lulled by the steady drone of the engines.

"Clouds?" Dr. Quest said, rubbing his eyes. "Look

more closely, Jonny. Those are peaks covered with ice and snow. You are looking at the roof of the world—the highest mountains on the planet. The highest peaks of the Himalayas range from 20,000 to almost 30,000 feet high, nearly reaching to the edge of the stratosphere."

"Wow," said Jonny. "Are we going to fly over them?"

"This plane won't go that high," said China Bill, from the pilot's seat. "We're going to fly up *into* the mountains, though. I want to check out the area we fliers call Cloud Alley. That's the last position reported by my Short and my two pilots before they got lost."

The engines labored as the DC–3 climbed across the dusty plain, and then the little foothills with their braided streams like the veins on the back of a hand.

Soon all the Quest Team was at the windows as the DC–3 approached the wall of mountains.

"Maybe we'll see an abominable snowman!" said Jessie.

"Yeah! A yeti!" said Hadji.

The Himalayas were a jagged wilderness of ice and rock. Narrow green valleys wound in under and between the peaks. One of the most remote high valleys was blanketed with clouds.

"That's Cloud Alley," said China Bill, who was back at the controls. "One of my pilots, a Scot named Drew, claimed he had spotted a ghost plane here."

China Bill hit the rudder pedals, and the DC–3 turned toward the cloud-covered valley. The twin engines pounded as the vintage plane continued to climb.

"Ghost!?" said Jessie, waking up. Jessie loved ghosts and was determined to believe in them, in spite of all the scientific evidence to the contrary.

"Of course, I don't believe such superstitions!" China Bill said.

"Of course," said Dr. Benton Quest and Race Bannon together.

The valley narrowed and soon the plane was skipping along the tops of the clouds, which were like a range of soft white mountains, a mirror image of the jagged peaks of ice and rock that towered above them.

"You say this is a permanent cloud cover," said Dr. Quest, assembling his cloud-penetrating camera. "That's peculiar. I've never heard of such a thing occurring naturally. I'll set up my camera and we'll see what we can see."

"Don't bother trying to use the windows," said China Bill. "They're too small. We'll open the side cargo door."

Race Bannon nodded. "The DC–3 flies okay with an open door. That's why they are still used for parachute drops."

"It'll get cold, though," said China Bill. "You kids had better wrap up!"

"Kids!" Jonny muttered.

"Oh, don't be so sensitive," whispered Jessie from the cockpit. "China Bill is so old, he even thinks my dad is a kid!"

*   *   *

14

Soon Hadji, Jessie, and Jonny Quest were wearing leather jackets over quilted coveralls. Together they helped slide open the cargo door, filling the cabin of the DC–3 with icy air.

"B-R-R-R-R-IDGE FREEZES BEFORE ROAD SURFACE!!" said Hadji and Jonny together.

Jessie laughed. The Quest teens sometimes liked to talk in the secret language they called "Roadsign."

"Woof, woof!" said Bandit.

"Come here," said Jessie. She unzipped her jacket and stuffed Bandit partly inside. But Bandit didn't want to miss the action, and he jumped out.

Edging carefully toward the open door, Dr. Quest set up his cloud-penetrating camera and aimed it down through the clouds.

"Hadji, I want you to take responsibility for the camera. Make sure it's loaded and running."

"Aye, aye," said Hadji, holding onto the side of the door so that he wouldn't be swept out of the plane.

"Here!" Race Bannon clipped a safety line to Hadji's belt. "We should all be wearing these. Just in case."

He clipped a safety line to Jessie and then to Jonny.

"Look, there's our shadow!" Jessie said. She pointed down toward the river of clouds, to a dark image of a DC–3.

"How could it be our shadow?" said Jonny. "The sun is east, to our right. That plane is in the wrong place for a shadow."

"That's no shadow!" Hadji said. He pointed down to the gray image of the DC–3, following like a porpoise plunging through the sea of clouds. "That's another plane!"

"You're right," said Jonny and Jessie together. "Another DC-3!"

It was flying in the clouds, so that it looked gray and insubstantial—like a shadow. But as they watched, it broke out into the sunlight—a silver DC-3, just like the one in which they were flying.

"The ghost plane!" said China Bill.

"It doesn't look like a ghost to me," said Jonny. "I can hear the engines."

"No markings," said Hadji. "No numbers. It's as if it came out of nowhere."

"It's waggling its wings," said Jessie.

"That's the international distress signal," said Race Bannon. "We'd better go down and see if we can tell what's wrong."

"Careful! It may be a trick," said Dr. Quest.

"I'm going down," said China Bill, throwing the DC-3 into a steep banking dive. "Even if it is a trick, I don't intend to let that plane out of my sight until I figure out where that DC-3 came from—and what it wants!"

RACE BANNON GOT UP FROM HIS COPILOT'S SEAT AND JOINED the rest of the Quest Team at the open cargo door on the right side of the airplane.

"I'm not getting anything on the radio," said Jessie.

"Better PROCEED WITH CAUTION," said Hadji, lapsing into Roadsign.

"The kid's right," Race Bannon called out to China Bill. "I smell a trick."

"As long as we stay behind him, there's nothing he can do to us," said China Bill. His hands were steady on the controls.

The Quest Team—including Bandit—stood at the open cargo door of the DC–3.

The engines thrummed as the Felix Air DC–3 followed its unmarked twin along the line of clouds that ran like a foaming white river between the jagged peaks. Twisting and turning, the planes ascended higher and higher, into the mountains. Sheer walls of rock and ice pressed closer and closer on each side.

"We're deep into Cloud Alley," said China Bill. "Nobody knows what's under there. It has never been mapped. I hope you have your camera going, Dr. Quest."

17

"Affirmative," said Hadji. "Unless the clouds are too thick for the camera to penetrate."

"What would keep these clouds here forever?" asked Jessie.

Dr. Quest mused aloud: "It must be some kind of interaction between the cold ice and the warm air. Like the fog off the bay back in Maine—but permanent."

"Look up ahead," said Jonny. "He's turning down into the cloud!"

As they watched, the ghost plane made a shallow dive into a cloud.

Shouting, "Hold on!" China Bill followed.

"It's like flying into a pillow!" Jessie shouted.

"Or a cloud!" said Jonny.

"Woof, woof!" said Bandit from Jessie's arms.

All around was soft white. The wingtips could barely be seen from the open cargo door.

"Aren't you afraid we'll hit something?" asked Race Bannon.

"I'm following him," said China Bill. "I figure he knows where he's going."

"How do you know it's not a *her*?" protested Jessie. But no one paid attention. All eyes were focused on the shadow that was the ghost plane. It was straight ahead and slightly above, barely visible through the thick fog.

"What the . . . ?"

Something fell out of the ghost plane. It was followed by something else; then another and another.

"They're dropping bombs!" Jessie shouted.

"No, those are—people!" replied Jonny.

The ghost plane was banking and men were jumping

18

out of the open cargo door—men on short surfboards, twisting and turning through the air. They carried ropes and grappling hooks.

"Sky divers!" shouted Hadji.

"Sky-*pirates,* you mean!" replied Jessie.

"Woof, woof!" barked Bandit, twisting free from Jessie's arms.

"How can they do that?" shouted China Bill.

"It's a controlled fall," said Race Bannon. "At a hundred miles per hour they can almost surf through the air toward us. And if they miss, they're wearing chutes."

Turning expertly, the sky-pirates "skyboarded" through the air, releasing long, lasso-like cords with grappling hooks on the ends—

Thunk, thunk!

Narrowly avoiding the churning propellers, two airborne intruders clung to the right wing.

Thunk, thunk!

Two more clung to the left wing.

The two on the right wing were crawling back toward the open cargo door, knives in their teeth.

"They're trying to board us! Shut the door!" China Bill shouted from the cockpit.

Hadji, Jonny, and Jessie pushed—but the cargo door was heavy and barely moved in its slides.

A tattooed arm was sticking through the cargo door.

"Woof!" Bandit took a bite.

Crash!

Glass flew from the front of the plane; the wind howled. Jonny looked forward to the cockpit and saw

19

China Bill wrestling with two more sky-pirates, who were climbing through the smashed side window of the cockpit.

Dr. Quest ran forward to help.

"Stop them!" Jessie shouted.

A sky-pirate, complete with headband and a knife in his teeth, leaped through the open cargo door; he was followed by another.

Jonny Quest was knocked backward, off his feet.

"Woof, woof" yelped Bandit, leaping at the intruders' throats.

Jonny saw his father and China Bill in the cockpit, struggling with two sky-pirates. Fists flew and knives flashed. The plane rocked and rolled in the clouds—no one was at the controls!

China Bill went down hard. Dr. Quest reached for the controls of the plane, but a sky-pirate grabbed him from behind.

Wham! Bam! Whack!

"Dad!" yelled Jonny.

Meanwhile, Race Bannon and two sky-pirates were struggling in the open cargo door. As they grappled, the plane slipped sideways, into a steep dive—and all three fell out, into the clouds.

"Dad!" It was Jessie yelling this time.

"Woof, woof!"

"No, Bandit . . ."

But it was too late.

The courageous little dog followed Race Bannon out the door, into the clouds—and disappeared.

Jessie and Jonny ran to the open cargo door and leaned out, looking down.

Nothing but clouds. The two sky-pirates were gone—and so were Race Bannon and Bandit!

"Aaahhhh . . ." There was a groan from the front of the plane. Jonny saw his father struck on the head by the butt of a sky-pirate's rifle, knocked out cold.

China Bill was already lying on the floor of the cockpit.

One of the sky-pirates was in the pilot's seat, fumbling with the controls, while the other was tying up China Bill and Dr. Quest.

Meanwhile, on each side of the plane, huge blurry shapes were appearing. The clouds thinned and Jonny saw jagged cliffs.

"Stay down!" whispered Hadji, pulling his two friends back from the open cargo door.

"I have to help China Bill and Dad!" said Jonny.

"Negative," said Hadji. "Our only chance is if they don't notice us."

They hid behind the oil drums that filled the back of the plane. The two sky-pirates in the cockpit were too busy flying the plane to look in the back for a bunch of kids.

"Look!" Hadji whispered. The light had changed. Out the open cargo door Jonny saw jagged peaks streaked with snow, dark pines, and green valleys.

They were under the clouds!

Straight ahead, a field of ice and snow was rushing up to meet the hijacked plane!

21

5

MUCH TO THE SURPRISE OF THE THREE MEMBERS OF THE Quest Team who were hidden in the back of the plane, the sky-pirate at the controls seemed to know what he was doing.

The DC–3's twin engines throttled back. The rush of the wind diminished as the plane steadily lost altitude.

"Sounds like we're landing," whispered Hadji.

"There's nothing out there but ice!" said Jonny. "I wonder where—"

WHUMP!

The plane hit and bounced, then hit again, more softly this time. Outside the plane, hummocks of ice and snow rushed by.

"Looks like we're landing on a glacier!" Hadji said.

"Unhook your safety lines," Jonny said. "I've got a plan. Quick!"

Signaling for his two friends to follow, Jonny crawled toward the open cargo door. The DC–3 was slowing, bumping across the ice. "Geronimo!" Jonny whispered loudly—and rolled out onto the snow.

Just before he hit, he saw Jessie and Hadji following.

The three hit the ice and skidded—and landed piled up together in a snow drift.

"If that hadn't hurt so much it would have almost been fun," Jessie said.

Jonny looked at her curiously. "Aren't you upset?"

"What?"

"You know. Upset about your dad?"

"Yeah," said Hadji. "We all saw him go out the door. Was he wearing a parachute?"

"Negative." Jessie shook her head. "No safety line, either. He had hooked us up, but not himself. I saw him fall, and then Bandit fell with him. I'm more upset about Bandit."

"You are?" gasped Jonny and Hadji together.

"I'm pretty sure my dad is still alive," said Jessie "Look."

She showed them a small black box on her belt. A tiny red light on top of it was blinking.

"Dad bought me this locator a few weeks ago. My red light is blinking, which means his locator is blinking, too. They are set up so we can find each other through satellite phone."

"You mean, you think he survived the fall?" said Jonny, amazed.

Jessie shrugged. "Dad is an ex-S.E.A.L., you know, and very resourceful. Maybe he fell into a snow drift or something. All I know is, my red light is blinking, which means his locator is intact. I will find him."

She suddenly looked sad.

"But Bandit . . . "

A tear dropped from her eye into the snow. The three friends looked at one another forlornly.

The courageous little dog had been a big part of their lives. Now he was gone.

"Look," said Hadji. "The plane is stopping."

He started to stand up, but Jonny pulled him back down.

"Keep down. We've got to stay hidden. They might not even know we were in the plane. That leaves us free to help rescue Dad and China Bill!"

"And find *my* dad," added Jessie.

Jonny Quest peered carefully around the snowdrift. The DC–3 had landed on the smooth top of a glacier. It was parked in the distance, the engines stopped. Two snowmobiles were pulling up to the plane.

The snowmobile drivers dismounted and climbed into the plane. A third snowmobile hooked a towline onto the tail wheel of the DC–3.

"They're bringing Dad and China Bill out," Jonny said. "They're putting them onto snowmobiles, tied up and blindfolded."

Engines snarled and raced.

"They're riding off with them!" Jonny said. "And now the other snowmobile is towing away the DC–3!"

Hadji and Jessie stuck their heads up just in time to see a snowmobile towing the DC–3 across the glacier, backwards. It disappeared behind a low hill of ice.

Meanwhile, two other snowmobiles were racing off in the opposite direction.

The three stood up, no longer concerned with being seen. All around them were towering mountain walls, their tops lost in the gray roof of clouds that covered the sky.

In the distance, two sleek snowmobiles were racing toward the glacier's edge.

With Jonny Quest in the lead, the three teens ran to the spot where the DC–3 had stopped. Grappling ropes and hooks littered the ice.

Snowmobile tracks led off in two directions.

Jonny pointed toward the edge of the glacier. "We'd better follow these tracks and see where they are taking Dad and China Bill."

"And rescue them," said Hadji, jumping back down into the ice.

"So they can rescue us," said Jessie. "And help us find my dad." She patted the blinking locator on her belt.

The tracks of the snowmobiles wound across the buckled surface of the glacier. The airstrip had been bulldozed smooth, but the rest of the glacier was rough, with *seracs,* sharp ridges and blocks of ice, and deep cracks, or *crevasses.*

"Listen!" Hadji said, pausing at the lip of a crevasse.

Jonny and Jessie paused. From far below they could hear a growling sound.

"Sounds like a bear," said Jessie.

"Or maybe a yeti," said Hadji.

"Let's get going!" said Jonny Quest. "There's no time to waste."

They followed the tracks down an icefall made of precariously balanced blocks the size of houses. Below the icefall, the tracks straightened and led directly to the edge.

"Whoa," said Jonny. "Stand back."

The glacier ended in a sheer ice cliff. Far below was a green valley.

"Whoa, indeed!" said Hadji.

The tracks led straight off the edge of the ice. Jonny leaned over and looked down—at least five hundred feet!

"Where could they have gone? Did they. . . ?" For a horrible moment Jonny thought his dad was lost forever.

Then Jessie said, "Look!"

Far in the distance, Jonny saw two orange parasails. And under them, two tiny dots that must have been the snowmobiles.

They were gliding down toward a cluster of buildings in the center of the valley.

"They sprouted wings and flew!" said Hadji.

"We're going to have to sprout wings, too," said Jonny. "Otherwise, how are we going to get down off this glacier?"

6

"CAREFUL," SAID HADJI.

"You don't have to tell me," said Jonny Quest.

The cliff below him dropped straight down at least a thousand feet to the green valley below.

The first hundred feet were sheer ice. After that were narrow ledges covered with moss and alpine grasses. And below the ledges were trees—hemlock and pine, clinging somehow to the steep mountainside.

A rope tied together from the discarded grappling cords was wrapped around a ten-foot-high serac.

Jonny stood at the edge of the ice cliff, facing in. He passed the rope between his legs and brought it around to the front and back over one shoulder.

"Here goes," he said as he stepped off the cliff backward.

Rappelling is one of the most elegant maneuvers in mountaineering. By releasing the rope slowly and using friction to brake, a climber can descend in long, easy swoops, holding the rope in both hands and using the feet to "walk" backward down the cliff.

Hadji, Jessie, and Jonny had all learned rappelling and other mountaineering skills from Race Bannon.

As he lowered himself down, Jonny wondered if he would ever see the ex-Navy S.E.A.L. again. He didn't share Jessie's faith in the blinking light on the locator. It could just mean that Race's device had survived the fall.

And Bandit—gone forever! Even if Race Bannon had survived, even if they managed to rescue Dr. Quest and China Bill, Jonny couldn't bear to think of losing the courageous little dog that had accompanied the Quest Team on so many adventures around the world.

When Jonny hit the first ledge, he called up and then waited while his companions joined him. Then they pulled the rope down from the top and refastened it on another outcropping of ice.

Jessie led on the next stage, and Hadji the stage after. Soon the steep ice ledges were replaced by narrow little "alps" or meadows of grass and moss.

Each stage took them down another fifty or hundred feet.

As the three teens went lower, the air grew warmer. Looking up, they could see the enormous bulk of the glacier, dominating the valley, but they couldn't see the mountains beyond. The higher slopes were all hidden behind the permanent roof of cloud.

"It's weird, not being able to see the sky," said Hadji. "It's like living underwater."

Jessie joined him and Jonny on a flower-covered ledge near the bottom of the cliff. They coiled the rope and followed a trail down alongside a beautiful rushing cascade.

At the bottom was a small pasture, where a herd of shaggy beasts that looked like buffalo were munching grass and flowers around an ice-cold, clear little pond.

"Yaks," said Hadji. "They look like buffalo, don't they?"

"Are they wild?" asked Jonny.

"If these are wild yaks, then those must be wild bells they are wearing," said Jessie. She pointed out that each yak wore a square cowbell around its neck.

Jonny reddened, embarrassed. How could he have been so unobservant? Alertness was one of the rules of the Quest Team. Now that the team was scattered, was he forgetting everything he had learned?

He smiled at Hadji and Jessie with new determination. Now that the adults were either captured or lost—at best!—it was more important than ever to notice everything and stay alert.

With Jonny Quest in the lead, the three teens continued down the path. It was beginning to get dark, and they were relieved to see a light ahead.

The light came from a small cabin made of logs and stones. A lamp shone in the single tiny window.

"Let me," said Hadji, stepping up to the door. "I know several Indian dialects, and the language here might be related to one of them."

He knocked on the heavy wooden door.

"*Frai nodji pa loki star purdam thi resto pwak?* (Anybody home?)" he asked.

"Who's there?" They heard a woman's voice with a perfect British accent.

Jonny, Hadji, and Jessie looked at each other in amazement.

The door opened.

7

"WELL, DON'T JUST STAND THERE!"

An old woman with long gray hair, wearing a fur vest and a New York Yankees baseball cap, pulled them inside.

"You—speak English!" Hadji said in amazement.

"Well, I should hope so!" said the old woman. "I'm an Oxford graduate, class of fifty-five."

The hut was round and lit only by the kerosene lamp in the window. On a small table nearby sat a book. *The Poems of Lord Byron*—in English, Jonny noticed.

"How did you get here?" the woman asked. "I didn't see you come up the path."

"We came down off the glacier," Jessie said.

"The Growling Glacier? Impossible! It is forbidden to approach the glacier, which is guarded by the Great Yeti."

"We heard growling!" said Jessie, who was eager to believe in mythical creatures such as the unicorn and the yeti.

"I don't know about any Great Yeti," said Jonny. "All I know is, our plane went down on top."

"Outsiders!" said the old woman. "That's even

30

worse. Don't tell a soul. Outsiders are strictly forbidden here in Sharma-La."

"How do you know English, then?" Jonny asked.

"Everybody in the valley knows English," said the old woman. "All the young people, anyway. How I learned it is a different story." She held out a hand. "Name's Rose. You can call me Old Rose. And I'll bet you kids are hungry."

The three Quest teens shook her hand and introduced themselves, then sat down to one of the blandest, but most satisfying meals they had ever eaten: fried bread and boiled rice with yak butter, followed by a strong—and smelly—cup of yak butter tea.

The three were famished, and they ate heartily. While they did, the old woman told them her story.

"In the old days, the best students from the valley were sent to England to study science," she said. "That was B.W.—before Wallace."

"Wallace?"

"Wallace the Wizard, our beloved dictator," Rose spat. "When I got to Oxford, I found out I loved poetry more than science. Since I especially loved pastoral poems, I became a yak herder. I hardly see anyone up here on the mountain, so I hope you'll excuse me if I talk your heads off. Have some more yak butter tea? It's a Himalayan specialty."

"Uh, no thanks!" all three said at once.

She poured them all another cup anyway.

"Who's this Wallace the Wizard?" Hadji asked.

"Oh, him. He's the magician who runs the valley. Came here years ago, out of the sky. Outlawed science, first thing. Then he cast a spell so the clouds would never go away. The clouds protect the Little Lama, our spiritual ruler, so that he will never grow old."

"Spells?" Jonny asked. "We don't believe in magic."

"Neither did I until Wallace the Wizard came along. His magic works, though. The clouds coming off the Growling Glacier have covered the valley of Sharma-La for fifty years. And the Little Lama is still a little boy at sixty-five! Nobody leaves the valley because the only way out is across the Growling Glacier. And who wants to tangle with the Great Yeti?"

"He lives in the glacier?"

"She," said Old Rose. "She's the one growling and snorting out the clouds, I suspect. More tea?"

"Please, no!" They shook their heads in unison, but Old Rose poured them more tea anyway.

"So no one knows about the outside world?" asked Hadji.

"Nope, not since the wizard outlawed travel," said Old Rose. "I don't mind for myself. I've seen the world, or England anyway, or at least Oxford. I never even wanted to marry, since I never met a man who loved Lord Byron as much as I. But I feel sorry for the kids."

She picked up the poetry book. A smile played across her worn features as her fingers caressed the cover.

"Wallace the Wizard outlawed poetry, too, because it promotes creative thinking. If his wizard police found this book, they would burn it. But what do I care? I have memorized it all, anyway. Now tell me about yourselves—"

32

Jonny, Jessie, and Hadji looked at one another, and at the old woman sitting beside them on the dirt floor—and decided to take a chance. They needed help; they needed to confide in someone. And there was something about Old Rose—perhaps her down-to-earth simplicity—that made them trust her.

Hadji told Rose about how they had been looking for the lost pilots when they had been attacked by skydiving pirates. Jessie told how Race Bannon—and Bandit!—had fallen out of the plane, fighting the sky-pirates; and finally Jonny told how Dr. Benton Quest and China Bill had been kidnapped.

"Sky-pirates, huh," said Old Rose. "That must be the wizard's patrol, who are the only ones the Great Yeti allows on the Growling Glacier. I have seen them gliding off under some kind of orange wings."

"They don't seem to be looking for us," said Jonny. "Maybe they don't notice kids."

"Lots of folks don't," said Rose. "That could be to your advantage. The problem is, if your dad and this China Bill character have been captured, they'll be in town."

"Down in the valley?" Hadji asked.

She nodded. "At the High Castle. That's where suspicious intruders are taken. If you are spotted, they'll arrest you, too. But I have a plan to sneak you into town."

"What is it?" Jessie asked.

"Slow down," said Old Rose. "First we all need to get some sleep."

"Thanks anyway," said Jonny. "But we're not tired."

Old Rose gave the Quest teens yak fur robes, and they rolled up in them and closed their eyes, just to be polite.

All three were asleep in less than two minutes.

The next morning Jonny woke up to the *clink-clank* of yak bells. He sat up and looked around at the log walls, chinked with rocks and mud. It was several long moments before he remembered where he was.

Hadji and Jessie were still asleep. Old Rose was snoring away on her cot in the corner.

Jonny opened the heavy door a crack and looked outside. He jumped back. A shaggy face was looking in.

It was a yak. The great beasts were standing all around the hut, their square bells ringing softly as they nodded up and down. There were about twenty altogether.

"The herd is my alarm clock," Rose said, sitting up, still wrapped in her yak fur robe. "They know today is market day, and they love to go to town."

"They do?" Hadji was awake now, rubbing his eyes.

"Why not? They know I won't sell them," said Old Rose.

After a breakfast of rolls spread with yak butter and warm yak butter tea, they started down the steep, narrow path toward town. Old Rose led the way, and her yaks followed in single file.

Jonny, Hadji, and Jessie wore fur robes over their flight coveralls, so they looked like yak herders.

"It should be easy to slip you into town," said Old

Rose. "If the wizard patrol questions you, just pretend to be deaf and dumb, okay?"

"Huh?" said Jessie, grinning.

"It's no joke," said Old Rose. "The penalty for foreigners is pretty stiff."

"What is it?" asked Hadji.

"Death by unhanging."

Jonny winced. "*Un*hanging?"

"You'll *see*."

That put a damper on the conversation. Deep in thought the little party continued on until the trail came out of the trees on a high bluff.

Old Rose stopped and pointed. "Down there you can see the town of Sharma, capital of the valley of Sharma-La," she said.

The valley below was bright green, even in the dim light under the perpetual clouds. In the center was a castle on a high rock spire. At the foot of the castle was a lake, and around the lake was a small town of squalid huts and crooked streets.

"That big building is the High Castle, where Wallace the Wizard and the Little Lama live," said Old Rose.

"Darn," said Jessie, studying the town. "I don't see any phone or electric lines."

"So what do we care?" asked Hadji.

Jessie patted the locator device on her belt. The little red light was still blinking. "I need to find a pay phone and call a special satellite switchboard where I can get a message—or at least the coordinates to locate Dad."

"That won't be so easy in that little burg," said Jonny.

"There are no phones in Sharma," said Old Rose. "Most of the people have never heard of them. The only electronic devices allowed are the walkie-talkies of the wizard patrol—and you can be sure that they aren't going to let you make a call."

The path got wider and smoother and less steep, looping down the mountainside in long switchbacks.

Old Rose led the three Quest teens, disguised as yak herders, across the barley fields and through the low gates of the town. A dozing policeman with a walkie-talkie in his lap opened one eye and watched them pass. He seemed more interested in the yaks than in their herders. And more interested in his dreams than either.

"In our valley, yaks are sacred," said Old Rose. "It is forbidden to kill or injure them."

The town of Sharma was almost empty. The few people in the streets seemed friendly, but sad, as they waved at Old Rose. Most of them were old. Their faces were like the clouds in the sky, perpetually gloomy.

"Where are all the children?" asked Jessie.

Old Rose shrugged. "It's weird, but there are fewer kids in the street every time I come to town. Maybe they are staying inside. I guess the perpetual gloom is getting to them."

"I can dig it," whispered Jessie. "How would you like to live where you never saw the sky?"

The crooked streets ran between small huts and decrepit log buildings. Everything was very primitive. There were no neon signs, no electrical wires—and no phones!

"It's market day," said Old Rose. "There should be more people than this around." She caught the arm of an old man in drab robes. "Where is everybody?"

"Wallace the Wizard is about to make an announcement," the old man said. "The whole town is gathered under the High Castle, at the Reflecting Pool."

"Big deal," said Old Rose. "I just came to take my yaks to market."

"Hmmmmm. How much do you want for them?" the old man asked. "I might want to buy some yaks."

"Buy them?" Old Rose looked horrified. "I would never sell my yaks."

"Why are you taking them to market, then?" Hadji asked.

"So they can socialize. They like to come to town, like everybody else." She snapped her fingers and pointed, and the animals ambled off

"They can take care of themselves for a while," she told Jonny and Jessie and Hadji. "I'll go along with you kids to the Reflecting Pool."

"Good," said Jonny. "It's time we got a look at this Wallace the Wizard."

8

THE HIGH CASTLE DOMINATED THE TOWN. IT STOOD A HUNDRED feet high on a rock, and the smooth stone walls soared up another hundred feet. The iron gate was guarded by two cops with walkie-talkies.

They both looked half-asleep.

The castle was surrounded on three sides by a deep moat, and in front by a square pond—the Reflecting Pool. At one side, the water in the moat churned down into a dark pit surrounded by sharp rocks.

"That's the Bottomless Pit," said Old Rose. "That's where the enemies of Wallace the Wizard and the Little Lama end up."

"I hope that doesn't include my father," Jonny said.

Old Rose didn't answer.

They joined the crowd by the square Reflecting Pool.

The town had looked so empty because everyone was here. The townspeople all wore yak furs and colorful hats, but they all looked mournful and sad. There were very few children, and they all sat quietly by their parents. They never played or laughed.

The High Castle had no windows, but there were a

38

series of ledges and balconies near the top of the highest tower.

"Oooohhhh!" said the crowd.

Jonny looked up.

A tall man in a high, pointed wizard hat came out on the highest balcony. He carried a boy on his shoulder.

The crowd gasped and applauded.

"That's the Little Lama," Old Rose whispered. "They're applauding him, and not the wizard."

"He's just a kid," said Jonny.

"Not really," said Old Rose. "He's almost my age, sixty-five. It's just that Wallace the Wizard's magic clouds have kept him from getting old. That's why people put up with Wallace and the cloud. They love the Little Lama and they want him to live forever. It avoids the confusions and hassles of reincarnation."

"Naturally," said Hadji, who didn't believe a word of it. But his sarcasm was lost on Old Rose.

Even though the Little Lama was the size of a ten-year-old boy, he didn't seem to weigh much. He jumped from the wizard's shoulder to the wizard's outstretched hand and then to the stone rail of the balcony.

"Huuurrrraaaahhhh!!"

He seemed to glow with a flickering light as the people cheered. It was almost as if he were lit with a candle from within.

He spoke in a high, musical voice.

"What's he saying?" Jonny asked Hadji.

"It's some sort of local dialect," said Hadji. All the members of the Quest Team knew several languages;

Hadji's specialty was the dialects of northern India and southern Tibet. "I can't make it out. Something about a spy."

"Two spies," said Old Rose. "He's saying that two spies have been captured, thanks to Wallace's wizard patrol."

"Uh-oh," said Jonny to himself.

Two hooded men in chains were brought out onto the high balcony. Even wearing hoods, they looked familiar.

Wallace the Wizard yanked off their hoods.

"Dad!" whispered Jonny.

"And China Bill," added Hadji.

"*Arpe se nomi creioplibam,*" said the Little Lama, and the prisoners were hooded again and led off the balcony.

"What's he saying now?" Jessie asked Rose.

"He's saying there will be an unhanging tomorrow," the old yak herder replied.

"He says everyone is invited to be here and watch," said Hadji, who was beginning to pick up the language.

"What is an *unhanging?*" Jonny asked.

Rose pretended not to hear. She looked at Jonny, shaking her head sadly. "Excuse me. I'd better go look after my yaks!"

The crowd drifted away.

Jonny and Jessie and Hadji drifted with them, trying to look inconspicuous.

"Now we *have* to find a phone!" Jessie whispered fiercely. "If I can reach the satellite number, I can get in touch with my dad."

"She's right," said Hadji. "We can never crack that castle on our own. If Race Bannon is still alive—"

"What do you mean *if?*" Jessie demanded angrily.

"I mean *when* we can locate him," Hadji corrected himself, "he can help us rescue Dr. Quest and China Bill."

"It's true," said Jonny, looking up at the steep walls of the High Castle. "It's our only chance. But where can we find a phone?"

At that moment a patrolman in a wizard hat strolled by, yawning. He wore a gun on one hip and a walkie-talkie on the other.

He yawned again.

He sat under a tree and closed his eyes.

Jessie looked at Hadji and then at Jonny. Jessie was the Quest Team's communications expert, and Hadji was a hacker and capable of operating any electronic device.

"Are you guys thinking what I'm thinking?" she asked.

Jonny and Hadji nodded.

"Zzzzzzzz."

"Let me do this," Jessie whispered.

Jonny and Hadji ducked behind a woodpile, and Jessie crept toward the sleeping cop.

"Zzzzzzzzzzz," he snored.

Jessie crept closer and closer.

"Zzzzzzzzzzz."

And closer.

"Go, girl," Jonny whispered to himself.

Jessie reached out stealthily. She slipped the walkie-talkie out of the cop's belt.

41

"Zzzzzzzzzzz."

Jessie turned and started tiptoeing away. She had covered half the distance to the woodpile when a sudden burst of static came over the walkie-talkie: *KZKZKZWKZKWK!*

The cop woke up, fumbled at his belt for his walkie-talkie—and saw Jessie!

He jumped to his feet. "*Al a braki stan!*" he cried, grabbing Jessie and twisting her arms behind her back.

"What's he saying?" Jonny asked Hadji—although he knew.

"Sounds like 'You're under arrest,'" said Hadji, stepping out from behind the woodpile.

"Wait," said Jonny, "Where are you going?"

"We can't let them take Jessie alone," said Hadji. "She doesn't even speak the language."

"Neither do you!" whispered Jonny.

"I'm a fast learner, though!" said Hadji. He ran across the narrow street and threw himself on the policeman's back, hitting him on the neck and shoulders.

"*Al a braki stan!*" cried the cop.

Soon he had Jessie and Hadji both in handcuffs and was leading them away.

Jonny Quest was alone.

Alone in a strange country that no one even knew existed!

He walked dejectedly down the muddy street, toward the marketplace. He didn't know where else to go.

What a dilemma! he thought. *The entire Quest Team has been lost or captured, except for me. One person, with four to rescue. This is the worst spot I've ever been in!*

He felt like crying, although, of course, Jonny Quest never cries.

Well, hardly ever, anyway.

He was wiping the tears from his eyes when he felt a tug on his pant leg. He heard a familiar "woof, woof!"

Jonny looked down. It was almost like seeing the sun.

"Bandit!"

9

BEFORE JONNY QUEST HAD A MOMENT TO CATCH HIS BREATH and greet the little dog with the hug he wanted to give him, Bandit began running. Jonny followed him through the narrow, muddy streets of Sharma, but could not catch him. As Jonny pressed through the maze of streets, he felt a strange mix of emotions.

He was thrilled that Bandit was alive. And he was mad at the little dog for not letting him pick him up!

"Bandit, come here!" he yelled. "This is no time to play games!"

But Bandit wasn't playing games. He seemed to want Jonny to follow, so Jonny did—around the corner, into an alley, up a narrow street, and down a muddy lane.

Whenever Jonny fell too far behind, Bandit would slow down just enough for him to catch up. Jonny was out of breath, but he kept going. He had finally gotten the message: Bandit was leading him somewhere.

"Woof, woof!"

The streets got even narrower and muddier as Bandit led Jonny Quest into the roughest part of town.

The only people on the streets were beggars and

thieves. Suspicious faces watched out of narrow windows as the boy and the dog raced by.

They passed through a wide gate in a dilapidated wooden fence, and Jonny stopped to look around. He was in the courtyard of an inn. Pack yaks and shaggy ponies with colorful saddles milled around in the mud.

"Woof, woof!"

Bandit was in a doorway. Jonny followed him down a steep stairway into a dark tavern, lit with smelly candles. The floor was strewn with filthy straw.

A few rough-looking men in fur vests and hats were playing darts.

One of them looked familiar. Especially when he hit a bull's eye.

"Race!" Jonny said, as the big man put his arm around his shoulders. "Can it be true?"

"Woof, woof!" barked Bandit proudly.

Jonny Quest felt an outpouring of emotion, and for the second time that day he wiped tears from his eyes.

But these were tears of joy.

"It's true," whispered Race Bannon. He had dyed his hair jet black and was wearing local garb. "Speak softly, because we are hiding out here. But where's Jessie? And where's Hadji?"

They sat at a table in the corner and Jonny explained how the two had been arrested. "She knew you were alive, because the locator was still blinking. She was trying to find a way to contact you through the satellite phone."

"Good girl," said Race Bannon.

"Then when she got arrested, Hadji made sure he got arrested with her."

"Good boy," said Race Bannon. "If they are just being held on some petty crime, they should be fairly easy to spring."

"We have another problem," said Jonny.

"I know all about it," said Race. "Your dad and China Bill are being held as spies in the High Castle. I saw them on the balcony this morning. I've been here in town since late last night."

"How did you get here? How did you survive?"

"I figured the skyboarding sky-pirates had parachutes," Race said. "So I just fell fast in a dive until I caught up, and I grabbed one of them. I knocked him out with a rabbit punch and sliced off his chute with the box cutter I keep in my boot."

"And—let him fall?" Jonny hated to see even bad guys die.

"No, I opened the chute and held onto him. Until I saw Bandit falling, too."

"He jumped trying to save you," said Jonny.

"Right," said Race, scratching the ears of the little dog under the table. "So I managed to maneuver and catch him as he fell by. Unfortunately, I had to let go of the sky-pirate."

"Ooooh," said Jonny.

"Woof," said Bandit.

"It was him or Bandit," said Race Bannon, shrugging his mighty shoulders. "It was kind of a no-brainer, if you ask me. We landed on the outskirts of town, in a rebel area, where I met up with these two."

"Rebel area?" Jonny looked around, puzzled. The two men who had been playing darts with Race joined them at the table.

"I'm Singh," said one.

"And I'm Drew," said the other.

Jonny was amazed. "You're the Felix Air pilots who went down last week!"

"Exactly," said Singh.

"Skyjacked by the same sky-pirates," said Drew.

"We managed to escape the hijackers, though they got our plane. We were on our way out of the valley when we made a discovery."

"This Wallace the Wizard character—" said Drew.

"This phony magician who is holding the whole valley hostage under these perpetual clouds—" said Singh.

"He's *Felix,* China Bill's lost partner!" Race Bannon put in.

"He wasn't killed after all," said Drew. "He's been ruling the valley of Sharma-La through trickery and fraud."

"But there is a rebel movement," said Singh.

"We decided to help them," said Drew.

"Me, too," said Race. "We are all trying to help the dissidents who want to overthrow Wallace the Wizard."

"You mean Felix the Phony," said Singh.

"Woof," said Bandit, who was always glad to be part of any movement for freedom and against tyranny and fraud.

"Count me in," said Jonny Quest. "As long as it means we can rescue my dad and China Bill!"

"Of course," said Race. "And Jessie and Hadji."

"Great," said Drew. "In fact, you guys arrived just in time. The rebellion starts tomorrow morning. The plan is to attack the High Castle and free all the prisoners."

"What about the Little Lama?" asked Jonny. "Are you going to overthrow him, too?"

"Not exactly," said Race.

"You'll see," said Drew and Singh together. "Let's go up the hill and meet our leader."

They left the dark little inn and walked up a dirt street that gradually turned into a rutted road and then a forest path.

As they trudged up the hill, Jonny Quest told the two Felix Air pilots how Jessie and Hadji had been caught by the cop.

"They won't be in the High Castle, then," said Drew.

"Where will they be?" asked Race.

"In the old jail under the market," said Singh. "That's where they keep petty criminals."

"Can't we get them out tonight?" begged Jonny.

"We had better take care of the High Castle first," said Drew. "If we attack the jail, it will alert Felix the Phony—excuse me, Wallace the Wizard."

"Hmmmmmm—" said Race Bannon. "But if we could smuggle some lock-picking tools into the jail. . . "

"Yeah!" said Jonny. "Hadji is an expert at picking locks!"

"Woof!" said Bandit.

"Negative," said Singh. "Faizu would never approve. Too risky. We can't afford to tip our hand. After the

High Castle is taken and Felix the Phony is captured, we'll be able to free everybody."

"Yeah, we have to stick to the plan," said Drew.

"What about the Little Lama?" asked Jonny. "He's the one the people love. Unless he rebels against the wizard, too, we don't have a chance."

"You'll see," said Race, with a smile.

The path ended at a cave. The entrance to the cave was strewn with flowers.

Drew stuck his head in. "Faizu? L.L.?" he called out.

"Come in," said a warm, deep voice.

Jonny looked at Race quizzically, but Race just smiled and shrugged, then followed Drew and Singh into the cave.

Jonny started to follow. Then he paused. Someone was missing.

"Where's Bandit?" he asked.

Then he saw the little dog running back down the path toward the town.

"Come back, Bandit!" he yelled.

Bandit ran on.

"Come on in," said Race Bannon, from inside.

"But Bandit . . ." Jonny's voice stumbled.

"There's somebody very important I want you to meet," called Race from deeper in the cave.

Jonny ducked his head and stepped inside the cave. The smell of flowers was almost overpowering.

10

THE CELL DOOR CLANGED SHUT.

The guard stalked off down the corridor, his keys jangling as he swung them over his finger.

"Now I see why there weren't any kids on the street," Jessie said.

"You and I both," said Hadji.

Jessie and Hadji had just been thrown into a huge jail cell with stone walls.

The cell was half the size of a high school gym. Blankets and cardboard mattresses were scattered around the floor against the walls. The only light came through a narrow, barred window at one end.

As their eyes got accustomed to the darkness, Jessie and Hadji could see the other prisoners: some were playing cards, some were sleeping, some were just sitting idly in the half darkness.

There were fifty prisoners in the cell, at least.

And they were all kids! Boys and girls, ranging in age from six to twelve, all dressed in rags.

"How could it be that so many kids in this valley are criminals?" Jessie mused.

"It's the adults who are the criminals," a voice answered.

"You speak English?" Hadji asked.

A girl of about ten stood up and walked over to Jessie and Hadji. She had flashing dark eyes and a gold ring in her nose. "Everyone in Sharma-La speaks some English," she said. "Orders of the wizard. My name is Arisa. Welcome to Market Jail. Where is your blanket, your pillow?"

Jessie and Hadji both introduced themselves—then shook their heads.

"Come, then. I will share with you. We all share here. One for all and all for one. You will learn that sharing is the only way to survive in this prison."

"We don't want to learn how to survive in this prison," said Jessie. "We want to escape!"

"We have to get out!" said Hadji. "Really!"

"Sounds familiar," said Arisa with a wry smile. "But you will also learn to accept your fate. Come, join our group and share our food."

When they were given dry bread and cheese, Jessie and Hadji were both surprised to discover that they were starved. They hadn't eaten since leaving Old Rose's cabin that morning, and now it was almost dark—although it was hard to tell in the jail, where the light was even dimmer than outside.

"This whole country's like a prison!" Hadji said.

"The wizard has turned our land into a dungeon," said Arisa. "Although most of the grown-ups don't realize it. We are here because we do."

"What do you mean?" Jessie asked. "Aren't you here for crimes—like us?"

"Wanting freedom is not a crime," Arisa said.

51

"I tried to steal something," Jessie said. "A policeman's walkie-talkie. I had to do it, but still, stealing is wrong; it *is* a crime."

"Some of us are here for petty crimes," said Arisa. "Playing is a crime in Sharma-La. So is laughing."

"It's a crime to laugh in Sharma-La?" Hadji asked incredulously.

Arisa nodded. "If you laugh at the phony Little Lama, it is. We laughed because we were not fooled. We took one look and we knew he was a puppet—a light puppet."

"A hologram," said Hadji. "Just as I suspected! That's why he's so light—and shiny! But how come the adults don't see it?"

"Grown-ups only see what they want to see," Arisa said scornfully. "The wizard had us locked up because he is afraid we will spoil his show."

"What about your parents?"

"Most of the children here have no parents," said Arisa. "They are orphans who lived on the streets. Children with parents are kept inside so they won't disappear like us."

"And you?"

"I had a mother, but she saw the truth also. She joined a rebel group and was killed by Wallace the Wizard," said Arisa. "At least that's what they told me. I never saw her again."

"I'm sorry," said Jessie. She knew what it meant to lose a parent. She had lost her mother years before, and now she didn't know where her father was.

She looked sadly at the empty spot on her belt. Her

52

locator had been taken away when she was arrested. She missed the blinking light almost as much as she missed Race—it was her only proof that he was alive and looking for her.

Hadji made his way through the crowded cell, to the tiny barred window. It looked out onto a trash-filled alley.

"Sooner or later Jonny will find us," he said. "But I hope he is able to rescue his dad and China Bill first."

11

"MEET THE LEADER OF THE REBEL MOVEMENT," SAID RACE.

Jonny followed him into a small whitewashed room carved from solid rock. It was filled with flowers.

In the center of the flowers, an old man with a long white beard sat on a block of wood, drinking tea from a china cup without a handle.

He had a bright smile and a merry twinkle in his eye.

If he wore a red suit, Jonny thought, *he would look like a skinny Santa.*

"Greetings," the old man said. "I am Domi Abulu, also known as the Little Lama."

"How could that be?" said Jonny. "I saw the Little Lama on the balcony with Wallace the Wizard. He's just a kid."

"He's a phony," said the smiling old man. "A light puppet."

"A hologram," said Race Bannon.

"So that's why he shimmered and looked so weird!" Jonny said.

"Exactly," said Singh.

"Felix the Phony—excuse me, I mean Wallace the Wizard—uses it to fool the people," said Drew.

"But it looks so real!" said Jonny.

"That's the problem," said the Little Lama. "Sit beside me. I have a confession to make. You see—" He blushed, embarrassed. "It's all my fault!"

"It is?" Jonny asked.

"Yes. When I was a young man, more than fifty years ago, the man you call Felix was brought to me at the High Castle. His plane had crash-landed and he had barely escaped with his life. I was only ten years old, already the spiritual leader of Sharma-La. But I was interested in the world outside, so I used Felix's scientific and mechanical ability to make my escape."

"Escape?"

"Yes. The cargo in the plane included a movie camera. Felix and I used it to make a film of me, and he played it on the balcony once a week so people wouldn't know I was gone. I went to India, then to England, then to America. Ultimately, I went around the world."

"You didn't come back?"

"Not for fifty years," the Little Lama said. "I returned only two years ago. I found that Felix had somehow managed to isolate the valley under a sea of permanent clouds. He had hijacked other planes and stolen enough electronic equipment to make my people believe I was still with them—still a ten-year-old boy. The wizard had stolen my soul!"

"He had replaced the film image with a hologram," said Race Bannon.

"A very clever hologram, powered by credulity," said Singh. "People see what they *want* to see."

"I found that Felix had turned evil," said the Little Lama. "Perhaps he had always been evil, and I had been willing to overlook his evil when it served my purposes. He called himself Wallace the Wizard, and he cast some sort of spell over the Growling Glacier to keep the valley covered with perpetual clouds."

"All phony stuff, I am sure," said Jonny.

"Don't be so sure, young man," said the Little Lama. "There are those who think he made a deal with the Great Yeti who lives under the ice."

"Has anyone ever seen this Great Yeti?" asked Race Bannon, who was very impatient with superstitions of all kind.

"No, but they hear her growling if they try to cross the glacier."

"Humph! It must be a trick," said Race Bannon.

Jonny wasn't so sure. He couldn't think of a rational explanation for the perpetual clouds—or the Growling Glacier. "I heard it myself," he confessed.

"Felix fooled and tricked my people, but it was I who betrayed them," said the white-bearded old man, with a sad expression. "I delivered my people to their oppressor. And all the while they have been faithful to me, in their way."

"Or to your image," said Race Bannon.

"So why didn't you just expose him?" asked Jonny.

"I was foolish enough to try. He had me locked up. Those who believed me, he threw into the Bottomless Pit. There were some children who recognized his deception, but they disappeared. I barely escaped with my life."

"But he never gave up," said a voice from the back of the cave. "We wouldn't let him."

A woman stepped out of the shadows. She was beautiful, wearing military fatigues and carrying a machine gun.

"This is Faizu, my rebel commander," said the Little Lama.

The woman bowed.

"A woman!?!" protested Race Bannon.

"Why not?" asked the Little Lama.

"Why not?" repeated Jonny Quest. *Sometimes Race was so old-fashioned!*

"She helped me escape from the wizard, and she has sheltered me while we plan the day of freedom. Which begins tomorrow!"

"How many guns do you have?" asked Race.

Faizu laughed. "Very few. Our rebellion is to be a peaceful one."

Race Bannon shook his head. "How can that be? Wallace has surrounded the High Castle with armed soldiers. He is planning to execute our people tomorrow!"

The Little Lama smiled. "Only a few soldiers, and we will win them over," he said. "My fifty-year odyssey was not entirely wasted. I saw enough of the world to learn that violence solves nothing. No, with Faizu's help—and yours, gentlemen!—I have a plan to dislodge the wizard and reveal myself to my people, without bloodshed."

"It is the only way L.L. will allow it," said Faizu.

"L.L.?" asked Jonny.

57

"That's the name they have for me," said the Little Lama with a smile.

"Are you a pacifist, too?" Jonny asked Faizu.

"Not really," the beautiful commando answered. "When I became a rebel, my daughter Arisa disappeared, and I later learned she was killed by the wizard. I would love to get my revenge. But out of respect for L.L., we are pledged to follow his nonviolent way."

"Whatever," said Jonny Quest. "As long as my dad gets rescued.

"And China Bill!" said Singh and Drew.

"And Hadji and Jessie," said Race.

And don't forget Bandit, Jonny thought, wondering to himself where the courageous little dog had gone.

"So! Let's go over the plan," said the Little Lama. "I was stumped for years, trying to think of a peaceful way. Then my two Air Felix friends arrived and showed me the way."

"Felix Air," corrected Drew.

"And we're changing the name, anyway," added Singh.

"Whatever," said the Little Lama. "Since the castle is impregnable from the ground, we are going to attack from above and below, simultaneously."

"Above and below?" Jonny was confused.

"There is a secret entrance to the castle, which only the wizard and I know about. It is through an underground cave near the Reflecting Pool. In the morning, when the wizard is on the balcony preparing to entertain—or horrify—the people with the unhanging of the spies—"

Jonny couldn't help shivering. He still didn't know what an unhanging was, but he knew he didn't like the sound of it.

"—Faizu will enter the tunnel with a squad of special commandos, ten in all. They will use the secret weapon to disarm the palace guards. Meanwhile, my air force will be heading for the top balcony."

"Secret weapon? Air force?" Race looked encouraged.

"As you may have seen, the wizard's elite guard uses parasails to get around," said Drew.

"They used them to fly off the glacier," Jonny said. "Parasails, attached to a snowmobile."

"Yes," said the Little Lama. "I don't know what Felix's soldiers are doing on the glacier, but they are up there a lot."

"Maybe they are feeding the Great Yeti," said Race.

The others ignored his sarcasm.

"We burgled the wizard's warehouse and swiped these," said Singh. He displayed three parasail chute packs. "These will get the Little Lama and us from the cliff outside of town, onto the top balcony."

"In just thirty-five seconds," said Drew.

"Only three parasails?" Jonny looked around the room. "But there are five of us here, not counting Faizu!"

"Three will be enough," said the Little Lama.

"It's all we could steal, anyway," said Singh.

"It was going to be me, Singh, and L.L.," said Drew. "But I'm going to give my spot to you, Race. On account of your S.E.A.L. background, cool-headed common sense, and general courage."

"I'm honored," said Race. "I am fully qualified with the parasail, and I will do my best."

"What about meeeee?" Jonny Quest wailed.

"I'm going up onto the glacier to find our Short," said Drew. "You can come with me."

"No way," said Jonny. "I'll join Faizu's commando team."

"Negative," said Faizu. "No kids allowed."

"I'm not a kid!" protested Jonny Quest. "And you're just as prejudiced as Race Bannon."

"Prejudiced?" said Faizu, looking puzzled.

"You're right, you're not a kid," Race said, speaking directly to Jonny Quest. "You are a full member of the Quest Team, correct?"

"Correct," said Jonny, hopefully.

"Then make yourself useful," said Race coldly. "Go with Drew up to the glacier and help put the Short together, so we can fly out of here when this is all over. And quit complaining!"

"And miss all the excitement," muttered Jonny Quest.

He was soon to find out how wrong he was.

12

OLD MR. YALA HAD RUN HIS LOCKSMITH STAND IN THE MARKET without any trouble for many years. He sold locks and keys of all kinds, and fixed them, too, some ancient and some new.

Most of what he had to sell was old and recycled, since the valley of Sharma-La had been cut off from the world for fifty years. But Mr. Yala didn't mind. There was no place he wanted to go.

Wallace the Wizard was weird, for sure, and cruel, and greedy. His taxes took all Mr. Yala's meager earnings. But he kept the beloved Little Lama young (and shining, as if he had just stepped from a bath), so the sacrifice was worth it.

It was getting dark; almost time to close. It had been a slow day in the market.

Of course, it was always slow in Sharma-La, where the sun never shone. People moved slowly, talked slowly, thought slowly—and brought their locks in to be fixed slowly, if at all.

Mr. Yala put his locksmithing tools away, nestling them neatly in their little cedar box. He stood up and started folding the awning over his

61

stall, when he heard a strange "woof, woof!" behind him.

Then a crash.

Mr. Yala turned around and saw that his table had been tipped over. His locks and keys were scattered all over the paving stones.

He groaned, but not too loudly. It was only a minor irritation. His neighbors would help pick everything up, and he didn't worry about losing anything. No one stole in Sharma-La.

Then he saw the funny little dog. Holding the cedar box in its mouth.

"*Wan ti!* (You rascal!)" said Mr. Yala, shaking his finger at the dog. "*Tra spo li!* (Give that back to me this instant or I'll wring your skinny little neck, you thieving hound!)"

"Woof, woof (No)," replied the dog, and shaking its tail, it ran off through the marketplace with the tools in its mouth.

"*Sermi top pwion vuska nemba tri portant se cramilani drem so prat yi gren squal dwian cro melli opo ferd siu pwes nix zoji pres lilli bonni!* (Grab him!)" cried Mr. Yala.

But Mr. Yala's neighbors, even though they tried to help, were too slow. The dog darted under tables, between legs, and out from under outstretched arms and hands.

"*Darran!* (Darn!)" said Mr. Yala.

The dog was gone—down the street and around the corner.

13

"THIS IS DUMB," SAID JONNY QUEST, AS HE AND DREW MADE their way up the mountainside toward the glacier.

Drew didn't say anything.

"A drag," said Jonny.

Drew didn't say anything.

"I want to be part of the action," said Jonny.

Drew didn't say anything.

"My dad always lets me be part of the action."

"Oh, quit complaining," said Drew. "You should hear yourself."

"Well, it *is* dumb," Jonny muttered. "And besides, aren't we taking the hard way? This sure is a steep little canyon."

Drew unfolded a map. "Faizu told me to take this trail to avoid wizard police patrols," he said. "This canyon is called Ode Layhe Who, or Late Echo Canyon."

"Wonder what that means?" Jonny mused

He found out a few steps later. "*This is dumb, this is dumb,*" came a whiny voice from above and below at once. "*Dumb, dumb, dumb . . .*"

"*My dad always lets me, always lets me, lets me,*

me, me," the same whiny voice echoed in and out, getting softer and softer as they climbed higher and higher.

"*You should hear yourself, hear yourself, yourself, yourself, yourself . . .*"

Jonny's ears reddened.

"I see what you mean," he said, as they trudged upwards toward the glacier.

At the top of Late Echo Canyon, Jonny and Drew stopped to rest.

Far below were the scattered lights of the sleeping town of Sharma—and in the center was the dark mass of the High Castle.

Jonny knew that somewhere on the cliffs on the other side of town, Race Bannon, Singh, and the Little Lama were preparing their parasails. He knew that somewhere below, Faizu and her commandos were preparing the diversionary assault on the secret tunnel.

And here I am, going to find a stupid airplane!

But there was no point complaining. And Late Echo Canyon had taught Jonny just how childish he sounded.

Far above the steep trail, the Growling Glacier loomed like a white wave frozen in time, as indeed it was.

Above it was the dark gray of the cloud-covered sky. Jonny couldn't get used to the idea of night without stars; it was even worse than a day without sun.

A steep, narrow trail led from the end of the canyon to the bottom of a three-hundred-foot-high wall of ice.

"How are we going to get to the top?" Jonny wondered out loud.

"According to Faizu, there are cracks and tunnels in

the glacier," said Drew. "We will hear the growling from inside the tunnels. If we always go *away* from the sound of the Great Yeti, the tunnels will lead us to the top."

"I've heard the growling," said Jonny. "In fact, I hear it now." From the ice in front of them came a grumbling, growling noise.

"The Great Yeti," said Drew.

"You don't believe that, do you?" Jonny asked.

"Why not?" said Drew. "It must be some kind of magic, to keep these clouds covering the sky, day and night for fifty years."

He started walking around the bottom of the glacier, where the ice and rock met. "It doesn't matter what I think anyway. Come on. Let's find a crack. If we reach the top by daylight, we can watch the assault on the High Castle from there."

They labored across a field of boulders. The growling noise grew louder until they found a blue ice cave with a high, narrow entrance.

"Let's boogie!" said Drew, lighting a pine branch to use as a torch.

In the glacier, the torchlight showed a smooth blue tunnel. Drew and Jonny hurried inward and upward; their breath made clouds that dimmed the flickering light.

A hundred yards in, the ice tunnel branched. The growling was louder to the right, so they took the left branch.

The cave continued on. And up. At each branching Drew and Jonny followed the tunnel that led away from the growling—which got softer, but never went away.

When they emerged on the top, the clouds above seemed almost close enough to touch. They were silver, spreading a soft glow across the top of the glacier.

"It's getting light," said Drew, snuffing out his torch. "Look how the clouds are beginning to shine. Let's scout around and look for the Short. I know it's up here somewhere."

"You go first," said Jonny. "I'm right behind you."

Even as he said it, Jonny realized how unusual it was for him to be a follower instead of a leader. He felt he was losing heart.

He was sick of clouds. He was sick of gloomy Sharma-La. He was worried about his dad, and Jessie and Hadji. Not to mention Bandit.

What if the assault on the High Castle failed? What if the unhanging—whatever that was—took place as planned?

"The plane!"

Drew's excited voice came from just ahead.

Jonny hurried to catch up, but Drew was already running back to find him.

"I found my Short," he said. "And your DC–3, too. And a lot more."

"A lot more what?"

"Planes! Come and see!"

They rounded a steep ice cliff and stood at one end of a bulldozed airstrip.

"Amazing!" said Jonny.

There was the Felix Air Short, and there was China

Bill's DC–3. Both were still intact. Parked next to the DC–3 was the snowmobile that had been used to tow it. But what amazed Jonny was what he saw behind it.

More DC–3s. Five of them. It was a graveyard of vintage airliners, all looking forlorn in the almost daylight under the clouds.

There was something wrong with the DC–3s, but Jonny couldn't tell what it was—until he walked under the wings, looking up.

The engine nacelles were all empty. The powerful radial engines had been removed, along with the three-bladed propellers that had carried these first airliners all over the world.

It made them like soulless corpses. They had wings, but no hearts.

"It's like a museum of DC–3s," Jonny said. "They've all been stripped but ours, and it looks like ours was next."

"And look over there!" said Drew. He pointed across the glacier to a crack beside the airstrip. What looked like smoke was boiling up out of the ice.

They approached carefully. "It looks like a fire," Jonny said. "A fire in the ice."

"But it's not smoke," said Drew. "It's fog!"

The steady stream of fog rose to join the silvery clouds above, replenishing them.

Near the crack, the growling was louder than ever, a steady thrumming.

Jonny knelt down and put his ear to the ice. Then he got up and started to run back toward the row of disabled airplanes.

67

"Where are you going?" Drew asked.

"To get the snowmobile," Jonny said. "Come on! I think we have solved the mystery of the Growling Glacier!"

14

"WHAT TIME IS IT?" JESSIE ASKED.

"Who knows?" Hadji said.

"Don't you have a watch?"

"Not anymore."

"The police took it?"

"I lost it in a poker game."

"To a bunch of seven year olds?" Jessie was scornful.

"Some of these kids are pretty sharp," said Hadji. "They've had nothing else to do but play cards for months. Now shut up, I'm trying to sleep."

Jessie and Hadji were wrapped in blankets, lying side by side on the floor of the big cell.

The stone floor was cold, but the snores that came from all sides told them that Arisa and the other kids were used to it and had no trouble sleeping.

Jessie and Hadji lay quietly in the darkness. They couldn't sleep. Both were worried, even though neither wanted to be the first to admit it.

But as Quest Team members, they both knew from experience that it is better to face fear than to try and hide from it.

"I'm worried," they both whispered at once.

Then they both laughed, at themselves and at each other. As Quest Team members, they knew that humor is an important part of courage. Laughter keeps the heart strong.

"We're both thinking the same thing," Jessie said, more soberly.

"Guess so," said Hadji. "What if Jonny gets captured, too?"

"Or lost. Or hurt," said Jessie. "He's the only one of us left. I'm worried about my dad. And I miss Bandit. If something happens to Jonny. . . "

"He'll be okay," said Hadji. "Jonny Quest always comes through. I know he'll break us out of here. But remember, we're not first on his list. First he has to rescue Dr. Quest and China Bill."

"Right," said Jessie. "The unhanging, whatever that is. So I guess the best contribution we can make now is to be patient."

"And wait," said Hadji. "And hope."

"And try to sleep," said Jessie.

She lay her head down on the stone floor and tried to think of happier times in the Quest compound.

The Quest Team was devoted to adventure and discovery, but the best part of every adventure was returning home; and the best discovery of all was the beauty of the Quest compound on the rocky coast of Maine.

Jessie's thoughts soon turned to dreams. She was dreaming of Maine, of the sunrise over the Atlantic, and of the seals barking out on the rocks.

Jessie loved the feisty little seals. They sounded almost like . . .

"Hey!"

Someone was shaking her.

"Did you hear that?" It was Hadji.

"Hear what?" Jessie asked.

"That noise!"

"I was asleep. I was having a dream. In the dream we were back in Maine, and I heard a seal barking."

"That was no seal," Hadji said. "And no dream, either. Listen!"

From the high window across the cell that opened onto the narrow alley, Jessie heard a familiar, welcome sound:

"Woof, woof."

At the same moment, a few miles away, on a high ledge overlooking the town of Sharma, Race Bannon and Singh were fitting the Little Lama with parasails.

"I thought it would have wings," the Little Lama said, sounding disappointed. "There's nothing here but a backpack."

"The 'wings' as you call it, come out of the backpack," said Singh. "You have to be moving through the air, so that the parasail can fill up. Then the ropes will enable you to guide it. I will be right beside you."

"Wait a minute!" said Race. "You mean you've never parasailed before? I thought you said you spent weeks preparing."

"Meditating," said the Little Lama. "Teaching my

spirit to soar. Where the spirit goes, the body will follow, will it not?"

"Don't worry," Singh said to Race. "He'll do fine."

"Oh, yes," said the Little Lama. "I look forward with great eagerness to the experience of flying."

Race Bannon shook his head. He didn't want to seem rude, but this whole plan was looking crazier and crazier.

The ledge on which they stood overlooked the town. Across the valley beyond it was the Growling Glacier.

In the distance, Race Bannon could barely hear its low growl—which the Little Lama assured him was the spirit of the Great Yeti, hidden in the ice.

The growling couldn't be heard in the town, at the bottom of the valley. But from the mountainside, it was a constant background drone.

Race Bannon didn't believe in spirits, or even in yetis. But the sound was real.

Must be the ice grinding over the rocks, he thought.

"Sounds almost alive," said Singh, nodding toward the faraway glacier. "Makes me think there is something to this Wallace the Wizard, after all. Even though I know he is actually Felix the big phony."

"He may be a phony, but he's a real phony," said the Little Lama. "Whatever you think of his magic, his evil is powerful. Look what he has done to my beautiful valley. The people of Sharma-La haven't seen the sun or the stars in almost fifty years. But good is more powerful than evil, so we will prevail. Don't you agree?"

"Certainly," said Singh.

"Whatever," said Race Bannon. But he had his doubts.

Singh finished attaching the parasail pack to the little holy man's back. He tightened the straps around his shoulders and under his legs.

"You will have these two ropes, one to turn right and one to turn left," Singh said. "Pull on this rope here to go down faster and pick up speed. This last rope slows your speed and your rate of descent."

"Delightful," said the Little Lama.

"The good thing about the parasail is that you cannot stall, like in a hang glider," explained Singh. "If you go too slowly, you just fall straight down, with the parasail acting as a parachute."

"Delightful," said the Little Lama.

"The parasail material is lighter and stronger than silk," Singh continued. "Once we get in the air, the canopy will fill and carry us down in a long swooping arc toward the town."

"And the High Castle," said Race, who was concentrating on the rescue of Dr. Quest and China Bill.

"Delightful!" said the Little Lama.

"Any questions?" asked Singh.

"Thousands," said the Little Lama, smiling. "The spiritual life is filled with questions."

"I mean, about the parasail."

The Little Lama shook his head.

He stepped forward and looked off the edge of the cliff, straight down into the grayness.

73

"I have a question," said Race. "How will we know when to go?"

"Faizu is going to release a rocket at the moment she begins the attack through the secret tunnel," Singh said. "Until then, we'd better just relax."

"Delightful," said the Little Lama.

"Whatever," said Race Bannon. He was more nervous than he usually was before going into action. But that was not surprising. He was going into the air with a man who had never been off the ground; he was attacking a castle filled with armed soldiers, without even a gun.

"It must be getting light," said Singh. "I can see the castle."

"Me, too," said Race. "But something has changed. What's that weird thing hanging off the top tower?"

"That," said the Little Lama, "is the cruelest of the evil wizard's inventions, the key to the unhanging. That's the Sky Dungeon in which your friends are scheduled to die."

15

"SO THIS IS THE DREADED SKY DUNGEON," SAID DR. BENTON Quest. "It beats that basement we were locked in before. And it doesn't seem so scary."

"Wait till it gets light, and we can see down," said China Bill. "I suspect it'll be scary then."

The two men were sitting in a tiny bamboo cage, dangling on a thin rawhide cord from the highest tower of the High Castle.

Dr. Quest looked down through the open slats of the floor. Either the cloud-covered sky was getting lighter, or his eyes were getting accustomed to the darkness; because two hundred feet below, he could make out the rushing waters and sharp rocks where the water from the moat and the Reflecting Pool plunged into the Bottomless Pit.

"I see what you mean," he said to China Bill. "I'd better not look down." Instead, he tried to focus his eyes on the horizon.

It was almost daylight. Far off, he could see the immense white bulk of the Growling Glacier, blocking the entrance to the valley. Above the glacier, blocking any view of the high peaks, was the dark roof of perpetual clouds.

"What's that noise?" Dr. Quest asked. "Do you hear a sort of growling, way off in the distance?"

The Sky Dungeon was so high above the valley floor that they could hear the Growling Glacier—almost.

China Bill cocked his head to one side. "Almost," he said, "but you have to understand, my ears are shot. Too many years of flying noisy old DC–3s. In fact, that faraway drone sounds almost like a DC–3 to me."

"I wish it were," said Dr. Quest. "On its way to rescue us."

"You never give up hope, do you?" asked China Bill.

"There is always hope," said Dr. Quest. "That's one of the Quest Team's fundamental beliefs."

"I envy you," said China Bill. "Me, I gave up hope as soon as I saw my old pal Felix—and realized how evil he had become."

"There's still time for a rescue," said Benton Quest.

"Yeah. But not much. Sorry I got you into this."

They both knew that in a few hours, when the town had gathered to watch, the rawhide rope would be severed, and the Sky Dungeon would plummet two hundred feet straight down onto the rocks.

"Oh, it wasn't your fault," said Dr. Benton Quest. "We enjoy taking on dangerous jobs. If Race were still alive, he'd figure out a way to get us out of here. The fact that we haven't heard from him has convinced me he is lost."

"What about the kids? You have a lot of faith in them, don't you?"

"They are very resourceful. I'm relieved by the fact that they've never been mentioned by Wallace the Wizard."

"You mean Felix the Phony."

"Whatever. I think they hid in the back of the plane and were never noticed by the sky-pirates."

"Do you think they will try to rescue us?"

"If it's possible, they will try. If it's not, they will carry on the work of the Quest Team. Either way . . . "

"Either way, you are a dead man," said a voice from above. "Thanks for informing me about these kids, Dr. Quest. As soon as I dispose of you in the unhanging, I will have them hunted down and killed."

"Felix, you vicious—" began China Bill.

"Wallace the Wizard to you," said the man in the wizard robes, who was leaning over the balcony, looking down into the dangling Sky Dungeon.

"Where's your phony Little Lama hologram?" asked Dr. Quest.

"Resting," said the wizard. "Recharging. Even electronic circuits have to rest at times, you know."

"Why don't you wise up and use your scientific abilities for good instead of evil?" said Dr. Quest.

"And be like you? Ugh! What a bore!"

"Felix, don't be a fool," said China Bill. "Cut us loose."

"Oh, I'm going to cut you loose," said the wizard. "As soon as the people arrive to watch the unhanging. Evil outsiders, dangling in the Sky Dungeon, then *unhung* and crushed on the rocks, cleansed in the waters, flushed down into the Bottomless Pit. It will be quite a spectacle, don't you think?"

"It's cold-blooded murder," said China Bill. "If you let us go and come back with us—"

77

"All will be forgiven?" asked the wizard. "I don't think so. Why would I want to run a stupid class-B cargo airline, when I can rule my own country?"

"These people don't want you," said Dr. Quest. "They want their Little Lama, not your stupid hologram. And what kind of life is it, when they never get to see the sun or the moon!"

"The sun and the moon are very much overrated," said Felix. "But enough chatting. I must go and have my breakfast. It's getting light, and soon people will be arriving for the unhanging. I'll see you both, for the last time, in an hour or so."

And he was gone.

"Loan me your watch," said Dr. Quest.

"What for?" asked China Bill, handing it to him.

"It has a second hand. Since I know the formula for the acceleration of a falling object, with this watch to time our drop until the exact moment of impact, I will be able to calculate the exact height of the castle."

"Why?" asked China Bill. "It will be the last thing you will calculate. And what good will it do us?"

Dr. Benton Quest looked at him, surprised. "Knowledge is its own reward," he said. "Besides, it will give me something to think about on the way down."

16

DEEPER AND DEEPER INTO THE HEART OF THE GLACIER THE snowmobile roared.

Jonny and Drew had found the two-seater parked in the DC–3 graveyard and cranked it up. Then with Drew on the back, Jonny had ridden in ever-widening circles until he had found a cave leading down into the ice.

The ice was smooth and the snow was packed. The snowmobile's headlight was hardly necessary. The walls of the cave seemed to glow with a blue light as Jonny drove deeper and deeper down the steep tunnel.

It was almost as if the ice were lit from behind—and then Jonny realized that it was becoming daylight outside. The wan morning sunlight that penetrated the perpetual clouds was now filtering down through the ice.

"Hang on!" Jonny Quest said, as he threw the little snowmobile into a powerslide, taking the corners faster and faster. There was no time to lose.

"Yahoo!" cried Drew.

It was exciting, almost like a toboggan ride—except that neither Jonny nor Drew knew what awaited them at the end.

As the cave went deeper and deeper into the glacier, the growling noise got louder and louder.

And Louder and Louder.

And LOUDER AND LOUDER!

"It sounds almost familiar," Drew said.

"WHAT?" Jonny asked.

"THE NOISE. IT SOUNDS ALMOST FAMILIAR," Drew yelled.

The tunnel leveled off, and then ended suddenly. Jonny skidded to a stop, shifted down, and slowly maneuvered the snowmobile through a low arch into a blue-lit cavern.

"Wow!" Jonny said, as he cut the engine off.

"WOW!" repeated Drew.

They were underneath the glacier, at ground level. The cavern was two or three stories high. The walls and the roof were ice, but the floor was rocky.

A swift stream ran in one side and out the other.

In the center of the cavern, three roaring airplane engines were bolted to a massive scaffold made of logs. They were radial piston engines from DC–3s.

Their whirling propellers pulled in a constant rush of outside air, and pushed it in a never-ending stream across the icy creek and up through the cracks in the ice to the top of the glacier.

"It comes out as—fog!" said Jonny Quest.

"WHAT?" asked Drew.

"I SAID, THERE'S YOUR GROWLING 'GREAT YETI!' AND THERE'S THE SO-CALLED WIZARD'S PERPETUAL CLOUD MACHINE!"

"RIGHT!" yelled Drew. "THE WARM AIR PICKS

UP MOISTURE FROM THE COLD WATER. A STEADY STREAM OF READY-MADE CLOUDS."

"NO WONDER PEOPLE WERE FOOLED," yelled Jonny. "NOW WE KNOW WHY HE HIJACKS PLANES. AND OIL AND SPARE PARTS."

"THEY PROBABLY LAST A LONG TIME," yelled Drew. Like most grownups—even young ones—he liked to lecture, so he added: "MOST OF THE WEAR ON ANY ENGINE OCCURS JUST AFTER STARTUP, BEFORE IT IS WARMED UP. ONCE AN ENGINE REACHES OPERATING TEMPERATURE, THERE IS VERY LITTLE WEAR. ESPECIALLY WHEN IT IS RUNNING AT A CONSTANT SPEED. BUT MY QUESTION IS: WHERE DOES FELIX THE PHONY GET THE GASOLINE TO RUN THESE ENGINES TWENTY-FOUR HOURS A DAY FOR FIFTY YEARS?"

"HE DOESN'T," yelled Jonny. He pointed to a flexible plastic line leading from the rocks under the ice. He followed it to a meter box, where it branched out to the carburetors on the three engines.

"NATURAL GAS," yelled Jonny. "HE HAS TAPPED INTO AN UNDERGROUND WELL."

"ALL HE HAD TO DO WAS MODIFY THE CARBURETORS," yelled Drew. "CHINA BILL WAS ALWAYS BRAGGING ABOUT WHAT A CLEVER MECHANIC HIS MISSING PARTNER WAS. SO THIS WAS HIS MAGIC—JUST SCIENCE IN SECRET!"

"MAYBE THAT'S WHAT MAGIC ALWAYS IS," yelled Jonny. "BUT I KNOW A LITTLE MAGIC, TOO." He crimped the line with his fingers.

The engines stumbled and sputtered—first one, then two, then all three.

Then all three stopped.

The silence was deafening.

"Wake up!" said Hadji

"Go away!" Arisa grumbled and turned over. She had been dreaming that her mother was alive and had found her again. It was her favorite dream. She didn't want to wake up to the grim reality of the dank jail cell.

"Wake up!" Hadji whispered loudly, shaking her.

"Good news!" added Jessie.

"Good news?" Arisa sat up. "What's that?"

"Rescue," whispered Jessie with a smile.

"Your friends have come?" Arisa scrambled to her feet.

"One of them," Hadji said. He crossed the cell to the narrow, barred window.

"The best friend anybody could have," said Jessie, as she and Arisa followed.

Arisa looked out the window and saw two little black eyes and a little black nose.

"That's nothing but a dog!" she said.

"Woof, woof," said Bandit.

"Sssshhhhhh," whispered Jessie, as she lifted Bandit through the bars, into the cell. "His name is Bandit. Watch how you talk around him."

"Yeah," said Hadji. "He's not super-sensitive, but his feelings *can* get hurt."

"You two are nuts!" said Arisa.

"Oh, yeah?" Hadji grinned. "Look what he brought us."

He opened the small cedar box he had taken from Bandit's mouth. It was filled with shiny lock-picking tools.

"Wake up all the kids you can trust," said Jessie. "It's almost morning. We have to try and get out before daylight."

Arisa was already walking around the cell, kicking every sleeping body. "Wake up, Omary! Wake up, Sisna! Wake up, Drina! Wake up, Goizu! Wake up. . . "

"Slow down!" Jessie whispered. "I said only the kids you're sure you can trust!"

Arisa looked offended. "We are all for one and one for all," she said. "We all trust one another."

"Good enough," said Hadji, who was at the cell door, bending over the lock. "Now let's see what these lock-picking tools can do!"

17

FAR BELOW THE HIGH CASTLE, IN THE SECRET TUNNEL THAT the Little Lama had built years before so that he could sneak out and mingle with his people, Faizu and her little band of nonviolent commandos were creeping closer and closer to the locked iron gate that led to the castle basement.

Besides Faizu, there were eleven commandos. Two of them were bare-handed. The other nine carried black instrument cases.

The gate was guarded by two night watchmen, both armed with submachine guns.

And both asleep.

"Good," whispered Faizu, hearing the loud snores. "We have to get their guns and their keys, hopefully without waking them. Then once we are in the castle, we will use our secret weapon to disarm all the guards while the aerial attack is underway."

Her commandos nodded—and followed.

Faizu's commandos had been chosen from the few grown-ups of the country who had seen through Wallace the Wizard's deception. They were all fanatically loyal to the Little Lama and trained in the use of his secret weapon. They were all committed to the principle of nonviolence.

And they were all musicians.

For this sensitive first operation, Faizu chose two of her favorites. One was a 300-pound ex-wrestler named Hark, who played harmonica in a marching band. The other was a 90-pound tarot teacher named Rachel who played harmonica in the same marching band.

While Faizu watched nervously, Hark and Rachel crept to within a few feet of the slumbering guards.

They pulled out their harmonicas and began to play, softly at first, then more loudly. An eerie song filled the tunnel.

The guards woke up—and smiled, and put down their guns. They began to sway sleepily from side to side.

Faizu stepped forward, reached through the bars, and took the guns.

"How about the keys?" she asked.

The guards turned them over with a smile.

"It works!" she whispered loudly to the commandos, who cheered softly.

The Little Lama's secret weapon was a song he had written when he had lived in Amsterdam. He had discovered the melody while meditating. It made everyone who heard it peaceful—at least while it was playing.

The plan was to set up an orchestra on the first floor, and blast the music through the entire castle.

Faizu unlocked the door and the commandos slipped through one by one.

"Wait for me," she said. She went to the window and stuck a rocket through the bars so that it pointed up toward the cloud-covered sky.

"We have to let the Little Lama know we are inside," she whispered. "Anybody got a match?"

Daylight was creeping up on the hidden valley of Sharma-La.

Far below, Race Bannon could see the High Castle and the little bamboo cage hanging from the highest parapet.

It was still too dark to see who was inside the Sky Dungeon, but Race knew: his boss, Dr. Benton Quest, and China Bill.

If they were going to be rescued from a horrible fate, Race and Singh and the Little Lama would have to move—and soon.

But they couldn't move until they saw the signal.

"Wonder what's taking Faizu so long?" Race muttered. "And what is this secret weapon, anyway?"

"It's a secret," said the Little Lama. He was sitting on the edge of the cliff, his legs dangling over. "Be patient, my friend. All things come to those who wait."

"That's the problem," Race said. "We don't want *all* things. We only want *good* things."

"Do you hear that?" asked Singh.

"What?" asked Race.

"That—silence. The growling—it's gone away!"

"It has?" Race had barely been aware of the distant

hum. The constant noise had faded into the background. But now, indeed, it was gone. It almost seemed to make the world lighter.

"Look!" said the Little Lama, scrambling to his feet.

He pointed down the valley toward the town, where a rocket rose like a flower and blossomed over the High Castle.

"Faizu's signal!"

"They are in!" said Singh.

"They are ready to set up the secret weapon," said the Little Lama.

Race Bannon watched the little rocket, his heart pounding. He had taken part in many military operations, some of them very dangerous. This was to be his first nonviolent mission.

It promised to be the most dangerous of all. It all depended on a secret weapon that was a secret even from him!

But it was worth it. Not only to save Benton Quest, but also to help restore the Little Lama to his people. The more Race saw of the holy man, the more he liked and respected him. Restoring the Little Lama wouldn't get rid of the clouds. Race knew better than to believe in magic. But the Little Lama would be a kinder and gentler ruler than China Bill's demented ex-partner.

"Ready?" said Singh, as they lined up along the cliff edge.

"Ready," said Race.

"Ready," said the Little Lama. "But how do we start these parasails? How do we get them going?"

"Easy," said Singh. "We just jump, and the speed of the fall opens the parasail and fills it with air."

"I can't believe he's never done this before!" Race Bannon groaned to himself.

"Oh, you mean like this!"

And taking hold of Race's hand, the Little Lama stepped off into space.

18

FOR ALMOST AN HOUR THE PLAZA BELOW THE HIGH CASTLE had been filling with people. By seven o'clock, the faithful, the curious, and the bloodthirsty all had arrived.

The faithful were there because they wanted to please the Little Lama (or what they thought was the Little Lama).

The curious were there because the unhangings held at the High Castle were the only entertainment in gloomy Sharma-La.

And the bloodthirsty were there because—well, because they were bloodthirsty.

Dawn comes slowly under the clouds, and the milky light was just beginning to fill the valley when the gathering crowd let out a sigh of delight and wonder:

"Ooooohhhh!"

A rocket had gone off, rising from a basement window of the High Castle.

Spitting flames, it sped up and disappeared into the clouds. Then it exploded in a shower of light, illuminating the clouds from inside, as if they were burning.

The people of Sharma-La applauded.

There were more "ohhhs" and "ahhhhs."

They thought it was part of the spectacle. And in a way, it was.

Everyone in the street and around the Reflecting Pool was looking up.

No one noticed the manhole cover near the market that had been pushed open.

No one noticed the little shadows that slipped out, into freedom for the first time in months.

All the shadows were children, and all were dressed in rags.

Even if the people in the streets hadn't been looking up, no one would have noticed the children; for these were the children no one had ever noticed.

They were the street kids, the orphans, the runaways; the kids who didn't have parents, or whose parents didn't care. Or didn't care enough.

They ran through the market, down the narrow streets to the Reflecting Pool. They hid themselves in the crowd.

Hadji and Jessie stood at the edge of the crowd with their new friend, Arisa.

Bandit was by their side.

"We're free!" Arisa said. "Thanks to you—and you!"

She reached down and scratched Bandit behind the ears, just where he liked to be scratched.

"Woof, woof!" said Bandit.

"You're free, but we're not," said Jessie. "We still have a job to do. We have to find Jonny and my dad, and help them rescue Dr. Quest."

"If it's not too late," said Hadji. "Look!"

He pointed to a balcony near the top of the High Castle. Dangling from a parapet nearby was a bamboo cage with two men in it.

"It's Dr. Quest and China Bill!" said Jessie. "But how can we get to them? Oh, I wish Dad was here!"

"I wish Jonny was here," said Hadji.

"Woof," said Bandit.

A man in a wizard outfit came out onto the balcony. He wore a pointed hat and a long robe with wide sleeves.

"Wallace the Wizard!" said the crowd. It wasn't exactly a cheer.

Wallace clapped his hands and the bright image of a ten-year-old boy appeared on his shoulder.

"The Little Lama!" cheered the crowd.

"It's a stupid trick, a hologram," muttered Jessie.

"But everyone believes it," said Hadji.

"Not everyone," said Arisa. "My mom never believed it. That's why she became a rebel. I'm proud she did, even though I'm sorry she was killed."

"I'm sorry," said Jessie. "What was her name?"

"Faizu," said Arisa.

"Bandit, hold still!" said Hadji. Bandit was jumping up and down excitedly and spinning in a circle. He was grabbing at the leg of Arisa's pants.

"Bandit, be cool!" said Jessie. "Look!"

Hadji and Arisa both looked up toward the balcony. Wallace the Wizard was extending his arms wide. . .

"Not up there!" said Jessie. "Over there!"

91

She pointed toward the mountainside overlooking the town. Three dots were gliding through the air, coming closer.

"This is most excellent fun. It is almost as much fun as prayer," said the Little Lama. His face was creased with a broad smile.

"I didn't know prayer was fun," said Race Bannon.

"There are many kinds of prayer," said the Little Lama.

"And many kinds of fun," added Singh.

The three were having their philosophical discussion a thousand feet above the valley of Sharma-La. They were parasailing just below the perpetual clouds, down toward the High Castle, which was no more than a dot in the distance.

The Little Lama was as graceful as a dancer as he steered his parasail in long sweeping curves.

I've never seen anyone learn so fast, Race thought. *His religion may seem strange to me, but it is obviously the real thing. This man's faith is so strong, he can do anything.*

"Something's going on at the High Castle," said Singh. "I can hear the crowd by the Reflecting Pool cheering."

"Wonder how Faizu's doing," Race Bannon mused.

"Don't worry about her," said Singh. "She's the best!"

"I'm not worried about her," said Race. "I'm worried

about us! If she doesn't keep the wizard's guards occupied down below, we're dead meat as soon as we hit the castle."

"Not me," laughed the Little Lama. "I'm a vegetarian."

"Follow me!" said Faizu, as she sprinted up the wide stone stairs from the basement of the High Castle. Holding their instrument cases tightly, the commandos followed.

At the top of the stairs was a heavy wooden door. Faizu shot off the lock with one of the guns she had taken from the tunnel guards, and she and her commandos poured through into the castle's main lobby.

The castle guards had heard the shots; they had retreated to the hall. Faizu could hear their confused, frightened voices. "Who are these armed intruders? How did they get into the castle?"

"So far so good," said Faizu. "Now, let's hurry and set up."

"Lay down your guns or we'll shoot!" cried the palace guards from the hallway.

"What if they come in shooting?" asked Rachel.

"Then we're sunk," said Faizu. She hefted her gun. *I wouldn't even mind dying if I could take a couple of them with me,* she thought. She hated them for kidnapping and killing her daughter.

But her hatred of the wizard and his guards was balanced by her love and respect for the Little Lama.

"No time to tune up," Faizu said to her musical commandos, who were taking their violins, cellos, and horns out of their cases. "Start playing—the 'Secret Weapon Suite.' We do this L.L.'s way. One. Two. Three—"

And it had better work! she thought.

"What *are* you doing?" shouted Race Bannon. "What's with the holding pattern?"

"I'm meditating," said the Little Lama. They were still several hundred yards away from the High Castle, but the Little Lama was circling in one spot.

"There's no time to waste!" said Race Bannon. "We have to hit the balcony before that nutty wizard cuts the cord and drops my friends onto the rocks."

But the Little Lama didn't hear; or didn't seem to hear.

"We have to do it L.L.'s way," said Singh. "Maybe he's praying for the clouds to go away and the sun to appear."

"Well, if we lose much more altitude, we won't be able to hit the top balcony," said Race. "And if we lose much more time, it'll be too late to save Dr. Quest and China Bill."

"The prayer must be working," said Singh. "I see a hole in the clouds!"

Race Bannon looked up toward the glacier. He was surprised to see a small patch of blue.

"Whatever," he said. "But this is no time to admire the scenery."

Just then the Little Lama, smiling happily, pulled the cord that tipped his parasail into a dive, toward the High Castle.

"Geronimo!"

"Isn't this fun?"

China Bill and Dr. Benton Quest shook their heads.

"Oh, don't be such spoil sports," said Wallace the Wizard (or Felix the Phony, depending on your point of view).

Wallace was standing on the balcony, overlooking the Sky Dungeon, which hung by a rawhide cord from the nearby parapet.

Standing on the balcony beside him, waving at the people around the Reflecting Pool far below, was the virtual Little Lama—a holographic image. The image waved, and the people below cheered and waved back.

The louder they cheered, the brighter the Little Lama grew.

"Fools!" muttered China Bill.

"That holograph," said Dr. Quest. "What powers it?"

Felix/Wallace proudly held up a dish antenna. "Cheers," he said. "The credulity of the people sets up an audio wave, which I capture and digitize into an image of what they want to see most," he explained. "The source of the Little Lama is their own desire for a Little Lama. Thus I use their own desires to dominate them. Pretty clever, huh?"

"Diabolical," said Dr. Benton Quest. "Why not use your genius for good?"

"Why should I," asked the wizard, "when evil is so much more fun?"

"You can kill us if you want," said China Bill. "But sooner or later the people will see through your phony show. You're just like the Wizard of Oz."

"Hey, thanks!" Felix the Phony looked pleased. "He didn't do so badly. But excuse me, we're running late. Much as I love to chat, it's time to begin the unhanging."

He opened his arms and addressed the crowd in a loud voice.

"Greetings, good people of Sharma-La! As your great wizard, I welcome you. And as the regent and guardian of your beloved Little Lama, I thank you for your devotion."

The image of the Little Lama held up a hand, and the people cheered.

The image got brighter and more solid.

"Due to the ministrations of my magic, you will notice that your Little Lama has not aged a single day in fifty years. He thanks you for the faithfulness that has kept him young."

("And the credulity!" the wizard added in a sarcastic whisper aimed at Dr. Quest and China Bill.)

"The eternal youth of the Little Lama is protected by the eternal roof of clouds, a gift of the Growling Glacier that guards Sharma-La from the corrupting influences of the outside world."

The people by the Reflecting Pool cheered. The

image of the Little Lama grew even brighter as the dish antenna picked up the cheers and converted them to a holographic image.

"Outside influences are *always* corrupt influences. That is why today we must inflict the ultimate penalty of the unhanging on these two foreigners who dared to trespass in Sharma-La."

With one hand the wizard pointed at the bamboo cage dangling from the parapet.

With his other hand, he pulled a large rat from the pocket of his robe. He held it up by the tail.

"Therefore," he said, "I have invited my fellow wizard, Roderick the Rodent—"

"That's a real rat, not a hologram!" said China Bill.

"He's mad!" said Dr. Quest. "It was useless to try and reason with him."

The wizard held the rat high and then dropped him down into the loose sleeve of his cloak.

The crowd went, "Aaaaaahhhh!"

The wizard held his other arm out toward the cord that held the bamboo Sky Dungeon.

The rat's whiskers emerged from the outstretched sleeve.

"Ooooohhhhh!" cried the crowd.

The rat's tiny black nose and tiny black eyes emerged.

"Go," said Wallace.

The rat jumped across to the rawhide cord—and began to gnaw on it hungrily.

"Pardon his manners," Wallace said to Dr. Quest and China Bill. "He hasn't eaten for several days."

97

The crowd began to chant with excitement.

The holographic Little Lama was holding up his hands as if to bless the unhanging.

But amid the cheers there came a new chant, a high-pitched chant, growing louder and louder:

"Phony, phony, phony!"

19

"WHY DOESN'T SOMEBODY SHUT THOSE KIDS UP!"

"Street trash!"

"Who are they calling a phony?"

"Get them out of here!"

"Ragamuffins! The wizard should . . . "

Hadji and Jessie were running through the crowd, trying to get to the base of the High Castle, at the edge of the Reflecting Pool.

They could see that in seconds the rat would chew through the rawhide cord, and the Sky Dungeon would plummet to the rocks and into the Bottomless Pit.

Unhung.

"If only Dad were here!" Jessie wailed. "He would know what to do!"

"Maybe he is," said Hadji, shading his eyes and looking up. "Maybe he does know what to do."

"What?"

"Look up—"

*   *   *

"So long, Benton," said China Bill. "Sorry I got you in such a fix."

"It's okay," said Dr. Quest. "Thanks for helping to pass the time by reciting those poems."

"I love Lord Byron," said China Bill. "I know all his poems by heart."

"That part was fun, anyway," said Dr. Quest. "I just hope the kids are okay."

He looked up. The rat was chewing busily on the rawhide cord.

The cord began stretching.

Streeeetching, streeeeeetchiiiing—

The crowd below was grumbling as the childish chant grew louder.

"Phony! Phony! Phony!"

The image of the Little Lama started to flicker.

"Those stupid street urchins!" muttered Wallace the Phony. "How did they get out of jail? They're spoiling my hologram!"

He reached down to adjust the gain on the dish antenna. Just as he did, a shadow fell across the balcony.

A *shadow?* There were no shadows in a land with no sun!

The phony wizard looked up.

A winged shadow flashed across his mean, skinny hatchet face.

And another.

And another.

Just then, a sudden beam of light streamed through a hole in the clouds, hitting the balcony.

The evil wizard of Sharma-La covered his eyes. The crowd below picked up the chant, shouting, "Phony! phony! phony!" as the image of the Little Lama began to dim in the light.

The rat just kept on chewing.

"Eat faster!" shouted the wizard.

Another shadow crossed the balcony, and Wallace looked up—just in time to see the heavy boots of Race Bannon descending toward his face.

"Demons from hell!" Wallace shouted.

"*You* are the demon!" said Singh as he landed on the balcony. He reached down and unplugged the holographic projector from the dish antenna.

The Little Lama disappeared—

Just as the *real* Little Lama landed gracefully on the balcony, in the exact spot where the image had stood!

The wizard ran off the balcony. He stopped in the doorway just long enough to glare back with disgust and rage at China Bill and Dr. Quest.

Still unconcerned, the rat took his last bite.

"Just in time!" said Dr. Benton Quest, when he saw Race Bannon and the two other parasailors swoop in from the sky.

The three hit the balcony, their boots and sandals scraping across the stone.

A cheer went up from the crowd below.

"Saved!" said China Bill. "I never thought . . . "

Just then, the cord broke.

And the Sky Dungeon began to drop.

Faster and faster it fell.

"Oooooh!" gasped the crowd.

"Nooooo—" gasped China Bill.

Dr. Quest was studying the second hand of China Bill's watch.

Race Bannon heard Singh and the Little Lama land safely behind him on the balcony.

The wizard was fleeing, but Race let him go. He had other things to worry about.

He ran to the edge of the balcony overlooking the Sky Dungeon. He leaned out and reached for the rawhide cord, planning to pull the whole assembly in so that he could open the cage and rescue its occupants.

But he saw with horror that he was too late.

The cord had snapped.

The Sky Dungeon was already falling toward the rocks.

Hardly pausing to think, with lightning fast reflexes, Race Bannon vaulted over the railing and into the air.

His parasail streamed behind him, tangled. Race didn't mind. He didn't want it to open, not yet.

He needed to fall fast, if he was to have a chance of catching up with the plummeting bamboo cage!

* * *

102

"Dad!" shouted Jessie.

She watched in horror as her father jumped off the high balcony, right behind the Sky Dungeon.

He fell . . .

Then at the last possible moment, he grabbed the top of the cage in one powerful arm—and opened his parasail with the other.

"It's too late!" cried Jessie. They were only fifty feet above the rocks, and still falling fast—too fast.

"Nice try, Race," said Dr. Benton Quest. "But that parasail can't hold three of us. Let us go and save yourself!"

"It will slow our fall a little," gasped Race.

"The rocks—!" China Bill exclaimed.

"And it will steer us a little!" said Race Bannon, tugging on the steering rope with his teeth.

The parasail had just enough lift to carry the plummeting threesome over the rocks—and into the calmer water of the Reflecting Pool.

SPLASSSSHH!

The pond was deep—luckily—because Race hit so hard that he almost got stuck in the mud at the bottom.

If it had been rock— he thought, as he clawed his way toward the surface.

The bamboo cage had broken the fall of Dr. Benton Quest and China Bill—and then shattered to pieces so that they could easily swim ashore.

The three men surfaced in a blaze of light, and an

ocean of cheers. The townspeople around the Reflecting Pool were applauding, and Race Bannon blushed, thinking they were cheering his last-minute rescue.

Then he noticed that everyone was looking up.

"Why's the sky so bright?" he wondered. Looking up, he saw that the sky was only half covered with clouds.

The people were applauding the sun, which they were seeing for the first time in over fifty years.

It was shining on the top balcony of the High Castle, on the *real* Little Lama, who stood welcoming its rays with his arms outspread.

The clouds were almost gone, and the blue sky was as bright as a new car.

It was beautiful!

But the most beautiful thing Race Bannon saw was the weeping face that welcomed him when he stumbled ashore right after Dr. Quest and China Bill.

His daughter, Jessie!

"You're safe!" they both yelled at once, as they fell into one another's arms. Hadji and Dr. Quest joined them, while China Bill looked on, laughing, and Bandit leaped in circles around them.

"Woof, woof!"

Dr. Benton Quest was the first to pull away, with a puzzled look.

"Where's Jonny?" he asked.

China Bill looked up at the High Castle. "And what happened to Felix the Phony, the so-called wizard?"

*　　*　　*

"Darn!"

Singh rarely cursed. Darn was the worst word he knew. But it would have to do.

He had almost captured Felix the Phony, but the evil wizard had managed to retreat into the tower, locking the door behind him.

Singh kicked the door. Hard.

Then harder.

"No violence, my friend," said the Little Lama with a smile.

"We can't let him get away!" said Singh.

"Don't worry, he will take care of himself," said the Little Lama. "Evil is its own worst enemy."

"Philosophy is one thing," said Singh, kicking the door again. "But this is real life. We can't let such a vicious dictator get away scot free."

"Speaking of Scots," said the Little Lama. "Isn't that your friend?"

He pointed toward the glacier. Soaring down off it, toward the town, was a snowmobile under a giant billowing parasail.

Two tiny figures on the snowmobile waved.

The crowd below cheered as the strange craft approached the High Castle.

Then the crowd groaned, pointing up.

Singh turned. The sun was bright, and he wished he had the sunglasses he always wore when he flew his beloved Short.

Shading his eyes with his hand, he saw a hideous but familiar figure standing atop the highest narrow pointed roof of the High Castle.

It was Wallace/Felix. And he was holding a double-barreled shotgun!

"Felix the Finished," whispered Singh hopefully.

"Come down!" shouted the Little Lama. "All is forgiven!"

"Forgiven?" screamed the demented wizard. "I don't want forgiveness. I want revenge!"

Soaring up into a long turn, the parasail-equipped snowmobile began to approach the High Castle.

Balancing on his tiptoes on the narrow roof, Wallace raised the gun and aimed it—not at the Little Lama, who stood gleaming like a golden idol in the unfamiliar sunlight, but at the approaching snowmobile.

Controlling his flight with the long cords, the pilot of the odd craft went into a long graceful turn, and began circling the High Castle.

The wizard tracked the flight with the twin barrels of the shotgun—turning around and around.

"Oh, dear," said the Little Lama. "He's going to get dizzy and fall!"

"Good riddance!" whispered Singh.

BAROOM! BAROOM!

"Here's Jonny!" cried Jessie.

"But who's that with him?" cried Hadji. "And what kind of weird aircraft is that?"

"That's Drew, one of my lost pilots," said China Bill. "And the craft is a snowmobile with a parasail. Pretty clever, really. They used it to get us down off the glacier when we were captured."

"But what's Jonny been doing on the glacier?" asked Dr. Benton Quest. Then he looked up at the clear blue sky and a light of understanding dawned in his eyes. "Good boy!"

"Look!" said Jessie. "That stupid wizard is on top of the castle. With a gun!"

"Jonny is circling the castle," said Race.

"The wizard is going to shoot him," said Hadji.

"He's turning, trying to take aim," said China Bill.

"Jonny's making him dizzy!" said Dr. Quest.

"He's firing. . . "

BAROOM! BAROOM!

"He's falling!"

"Eeeeeeeeee!" went the crowd, either from joy or horror; it was hard to tell.

"Into the Bottomless Pit!" said Hadji.

"Good riddance!" said China Bill.

"He's gone!" said Jessie. "The recoil knocked him off!"

"For every action there is an equal and opposite reaction," said Dr. Benton Quest, who never passed up a chance to illustrate a scientific principle.

But no one heard him. Everyone else had run off to meet Drew and Jonny Quest, who were landing the snowmobile on the grass, as gently as a feather.

20

"ARE YOU SURE YOU DON'T WANT TO COME WITH US?" ASKED Dr. Benton Quest.

China Bill shook his head. He smiled and put his arm around the woman who stood at his side—surrounded by her herd of yaks.

"It's time for me to retire," China Bill said. "Now that I've finally found a woman who cares about the same things I do."

"'I love not Man the less, but Nature more,'" said Old Rose. She held up her edition of Lord Byron's poems.

"It only took him seventy years," whispered Hadji.

"Shut up!" said Jessie. "I think it's romantic. They make a perfect couple."

It was several days later. The Quest Team was getting ready to board the Short, which was idling on the grass by the High Castle. Felix Air had been painted out, and S-D Air painted in.

Drew had repaired the plane and flown it down from the no-longer-growling glacier. He and Singh were in the cockpit, at the controls.

China Bill waved at them. "You boys can run the

airline without me," he said. "Just be sure and get our friends home safely."

"Will do," said Singh and Drew.

"Good-bye everybody," said Race Bannon. He shook hands with Faizu. "Thanks for everything."

"Thank my commandos," said Faizu, who stood with her arm around her daughter. "The castle guards laid down their weapons as soon as they started playing. And thank L.L., who wrote such a powerful piece of music."

"I think we should play it on worldwide radio," said Arisa. "And bring peace to the world."

"It only works for a short time, my child," said the Little Lama. "And besides, peace has to come from within the heart, and not through a trick."

"I wish we could take you with us," said Jessie, kissing Arisa on the cheek. "We need another girl on the Quest Team!"

"Arisa may want to leave Sharma-La when she gets older," said Faizu. "But for now, I want my daughter here with me. I am so happy that we are reunited, thanks to our little friend here."

"Woof," said Bandit.

"Me, too," said Arisa.

"You are all welcome here at any time," said the Little Lama. "Or we may come and see you, since we now have our own airline, thanks to China Bill."

He pointed to the DC–3 parked nearby on the new grass runway. On its side was painted Sharma-La Air.

"Thanks for everything!" Hadji and Jessie cried from inside the plane.

"It was actually sort of fun!" said Jonny Quest, boarding with his dad. "And I didn't miss all the action, after all."

"Woof, woof!" said Bandit, scampering after them.

Minutes later, the Short climbed into the clear blue sky over Sharma-La.

SCIENTIFIC AFTERWORD
FUTURE PARACHUTES

JUMPING OUT OF A PLANE IS TERRIFYING. WE HAVE A deep-seated impulse to avoid falling that is very powerful. Falling triggers the grabbing reflex babies display immediately after birth. It is so strong in us because even short falls can do great damage to us. We have large bones, and our heads are particularly vulnerable to impact. Imagine, then, what courage it takes to dive out of an airplane, miles up. Yet people do it for fun every day.

Gravity pulls all of us toward the Earth with an acceleration that increases our downward speed every second. Starting with no velocity, a second later you would have accelerated to 32 feet per second—faster than you can run. Falling freely, you will speed up until the resistance of air itself offsets gravity's acceleration. This "terminal velocity" is about 120 miles per hour.

Jumping out of a very high airplane—say, over the Himalayan mountains—worsens your problem. Air thins at high altitude, so it resists gravity less, and your terminal velocity will be higher— perhaps 150 miles per hour or more.

Parachutes are the only current way to save yourself. Ordinary ones operate much as an open umbrella would. Its larger area catches more air, so the

111

total air resistance acting on you is greater, and slows you. Most parachutes are made of nylon, an artificial fiber that is strong and light. The greatest danger in parachuting is not failure of the materials. Instead, most accidents occur because the parachutist gets snarled up in the nylon lines which connect to the chute overhead. This makes the parachute fail to open properly.

Sport parachutes, or *parafoils,* have a special component (the sleeve), which draws a parachutist upright and makes it almost impossible to get tangled up in the chute and lines. The next step in parachuting will probably come, as depicted in this novel, by adding propulsion to the chute itself. If jets can move the parachutist, then he or she can maneuver to land in a chosen spot, or even approach other aircraft.

The ultimate expression of this would be *air-surfing.* The board would have to be powered, with the feet firmly held to it. The parachutist would direct the board by riding it, somewhat as a surfer chooses the angle of attack on a wave. Most of the job of keeping the whole rig afloat would still come from a large parafoil suspended overhead.

The technical problems of doing this are considerable. If an air-surfer makes a wrong move, he or she could get tangled in the lines leading up to the chute. Once a chute starts falling, because it is not fully opened, the wind speed picks up. This makes it harder to untangle oneself. Free-fall time from five miles up is only three minutes!

Though air-surfing would be difficult to perfect, the

payoff would be to give us true control of the skies. Even so, it would be very difficult for an air-surfer to overtake and board a moving airplane, even if it were a slow, propeller-driven one like the DC–3. Air flow around the plane would press against the chute, probably fouling its ability to support the air-surfer.

Boarding a balloon would be much easier. Balloons move at the wind speed, so the air is calm around them. Most modern balloons carry their passengers in a gondola dangling far enough beneath them, so a boarder could slip in from the side without risking being blown off course by strong air currents.

If air engineering keeps advancing, exciting possibilities open up. Air-surfer races between balloons, or between balloons and mountain peaks, may become common. Endurance records for air-surfers dropped from balloons could lead to people staying aloft for hours. With our ever-expanding technology and our constant desire to set records and perform new feats, the possibilities for new modes of air travel in the future are greater than ever.

Dr. Gregory Benford, Ph.D.
University of California, Irvine